FOX
SWIFT

TAKES ON THE
UNBEATABLES

FOX SWIFT

TAKES ON THE UNBEATABLES

DAVID LAWRENCE
with CYRIL RIOLI

slattery
MEDIA GROUP

visit *slatterymedia.com*

The Slattery Media Group Pty Ltd
1 Albert St, Richmond
Victoria, Australia, 3121

Text copyright © David Lawrence 2014
Illustrations © Jo Gill 2014
Design copyright © The Slattery Media Group Pty Ltd 2014
First published by The Slattery Media Group Pty Ltd 2014
Reprinted 2015

National Library of Australia Cataloguing-in-Publication entry

Author: Lawrence, David, 1964- .

Title: Fox Swift takes on The Unbeatables / David Lawrence ;
Jo Gill, illustrator ; Cyril Rioli, contributor.

ISBN: 9780992379117 (paperback)

Series: Lawrence, David, 1964- Fox Swift 2.

Target audience: For children.

Subjects: Australian football--Juvenile fiction.

Other Authors/Contributors:
Rioli, Cyril, contributor.
Gill, Jo, illustrator.

Dewey Number: A823.4

Group Publisher: Geoff Slattery
Editor: Bronwyn Wilkie
Design and typeset: Kate Slattery
Coaching tips: Cyril Rioli

Printed and bound in Australia by McPherson's Printing Group

slatterymedia.com

FOX SWIFT
TAKES ON THE UNBEATABLES

CONTENTS

1

Paw Form

Fox Swift lay on his bed, lost in a daydream about football.

He smiled as he gazed at the framed photo hanging from the wall. It was Fox's all-time favourite picture, taken after his team's come-from-behind Grand Final victory over their crosstown rivals, the Dragons.

To Fox, it seemed like it had all happened yesterday. He got up and took down the picture for a closer look.

The Diggers had beaten the Dragons against all the odds. It had been an incredible team effort, but there were some very special individuals who had changed the fortunes of the football club. He had scanned the happy faces of his teammates so many times since, and never tired of it.

In the middle of the group of players was the Diggers' coach, Greg Scott. He had been a star footballer 40 years ago, but after suffering a serious knee injury he

Check out the definition of any words in **bold** in A Quirky Footy Dictionary on page 274.

had become a recluse and rarely left his home. Fox had somehow convinced him to coach the Diggers, and Mr Scott had done an amazing job, taking the team from **wooden spooners** to Grand Finalists in a single season.

Next to the coach was the champion Hawthorn footballer Cyril Rioli. Fox could not believe how lucky the Diggers were to have Cyril as their number one supporter—his training drills and dietary tips had helped turn around the team's disastrous start to the season …

Fox's thoughts were interrupted by his mum calling through the bedroom door.

"Are you tidying up your room in there?" she asked.

"Yes, Mum!" Fox yelled back.

"Are you sure you're not lying on your bed thinking about footy?"

"As if!" said Fox, quickly leaping off his bed and picking up a T-shirt he had tossed on the floor three days ago.

After then folding and putting away a pair of jeans, Fox decided he had earned a break. He hopped back on to his bed and took another look at the photo.

His eyes were immediately drawn to the two giant Sudanese boys, Samir and Chriz, who everyone called Sammy and Chris. They had never heard of—let alone played—AFL footy until last year, but with their incredible height, speed and agility, Sammy and Chris quickly became the best ruckmen in the competition.

Next to Sammy and Chris was the red-haired Paige

Turner, who always wore a helmet during games. She was a gymnastics champion who thrilled the crowd by doing spectacular somersaults after she kicked a goal—and she kicked a lot of goals! Paige was an exceptionally accurate kick, and could **slot majors** from any angle. She was so good that the president of the Davinal Dragons, Miles Winter, had tried to ban girls from playing in the competition. Fox was very happy he had failed!

Next to Paige was the Diggers' tall full-forward, Simon Phillips. At the start of the season, Simon had been overweight and everyone had called him 'Porky'. He would even hide lollies in his socks so he could eat them during training. But Simon had trained hard and changed his diet, and now looked and played like a **gun footballer**. He had kicked five goals in last year's Grand Final, and the Diggers never would have won the game without him …

"How's it going in there?" called out Mrs Swift.

"Um, good," called Fox, jumping up and shovelling all the remaining mess on the floor under his bed.

"You're not just stuffing everything under your bed, are you, Fox?"

"No way, Mum!" said Fox. He was now pretty sure his mother had X-ray vision.

Fox reluctantly began transferring the clutter from under his bed into drawers and on to hangers in his cupboard, but soon found himself looking at the photo again.

His eyes stopped on Bruno Gallucci, the Diggers' reliable centre half-back. Bruno had originally been a Dragons player, but Mace Winter, son of Miles and captain of the Dragons, had blackmailed him into playing for the Diggers so he could spy on them and **throw games**. Fortunately the plan had backfired, and Bruno had become one of the Diggers' best footballers.

Next to Bruno was the farm boy 'Mo' Officer. Mo was without doubt the strongest kid Fox had ever met. Even his muscles had muscles! Mo had broken his hand in the Grand Final after running into a goalpost, but it hadn't stopped him from playing out the remainder of the game. Mo had come off better than the goalpost though, which had snapped in two!

A SELFIE

Next to Mo was Fox's best mate, Lewis Rioli. Lewis was the funniest kid at school, and Fox started to laugh when he thought about the cartoon Lewis had drawn and sent to his family as a Christmas card.

Lewis was hilarious, artistic and an exceptionally fast runner, but he was hopeless at footy. Despite his lack of football skills, Lewis had played a vital role in the Grand Final victory by tiring out the Dragons' best **tagger**, Angelo Blunt, who was known simply as 'The Glove'.

Without a doubt the happiest face in the photo belonged to the boy wearing the white bodysuit, Hugo Trippitt. Hugo had to wear the bodysuit because he was allergic to grass, and as a result had been teased by some of the cruel Dragons supporters. Hugo was super smart and, despite being rather uncoordinated, had managed to kick a sensational grubber goal to win the game for the Diggers.

Sitting next to Fox in the photo was the most popular member of the Diggers Football Club—and she wasn't even a human. Joey the kangaroo was the team mascot who led the Diggers out on to the oval each week, and gave the players "high paws" after a win. Fox smiled as he remembered the game last season against the Colbran Cockatoos. The opposition's star centre half-forward, 'Jacko', had been about to kick the winning goal when he'd slipped on some of Joey's kangaroo poo and missed the goals completely. The Diggers had won, and, as Lewis pointed out, Jacko had been really down in the 'dumps'!

Suddenly, Fox saw something in the photo he hadn't noticed before. There was a tree in the distance behind the players and it looked like there was a head poking out from behind it, as if someone were trying to sneak into the photograph.

"It couldn't be …" thought Fox as he moved up on to his knees to get closer to the photo and squinted his eyes. "It is! It's … Mr Percy!"

Mr Percy had coached the Diggers for the first three games last season, and he was definitely the worst coach Fox had ever met. Once he had even forgotten to bring the footballs, and made the Diggers pretend to kick and handball imaginary footies to each other for the entire training!

The only good thing about Mr Percy was his collection

of giant vegetables that the Diggers had ingeniously used at training instead of witches hats, which the club couldn't afford. Fox was rapt that Mr Scott had replaced Mr Percy, and he couldn't wait to captain the Diggers again this year.

Fox's daydreaming was interrupted by the sound of the doorbell.

"I'll get it, Mum!" he called out. "It's Lewis and Jimmy—they've come to have a kick with me and Chase."

"Have you finished tidying up your room?"

"Yes!" said Fox, ignoring the giant mess on top of his desk.

"What about your desk?"

"She is spooky!" thought Fox.

"I'll fix it later, Mum," he said.

"My mother can obviously see through walls," thought Fox as he ran down the corridor to the front door. "I'll never be able to go to the bathroom at home again!"

Across the other side of town, the sour-faced Miles Winter parked his expensive sports car near a narrow laneway. His equally sour-faced son, Mace, sat in the front passenger seat and watched as his father put on a wig, a false beard and a fake moustache.

"That's great, Dad—even *I* can't recognise you!" said Mace.

"Good," said Miles. "No one can ever find out what we're up to—no one!"

Miles picked up a brown paper bag from under his seat, jumped out of the car and looked around suspiciously. Then, after making sure nobody was watching, he calmly walked into the dark laneway.

Waiting for him was a nervous-looking Mr Jackson, father of the Colbran Cocktatoos' star centre half-forward, Jacko. Miles gave Mr Jackson a sly look, then handed over the paper bag. Mr Jackson opened the bag and saw it was filled with money. He immediately took out the wad of notes and gleefully started counting them.

Meanwhile, back in the car, Mace was looking in the glovebox for any loose change he could pinch from his dad when he spotted his friend Vince approaching along the footpath.

"Uh-oh," he thought, ducking down so that Vince wouldn't see him.

In the laneway Miles watched as Mr Jackson finished counting the money.

"I told you it was all there," he said. "So Jacko now plays for the Dragons, not the Colbran Cocktatoos, right?"

"He sure does!" replied a very happy Mr Jackson. "By the way, who are you?"

"That is something you will never know," said Miles, with an air of mystery.

Unfortunately for Miles, it was right at this moment

that Vince looked down the laneway and spotted him.

"Hey, Mr Winter! What's with the fake beard and wig?"

"Shut up, Vince!" said Miles angrily.

Miles stormed back up the lane and told Vince to follow him to his car.

As soon as Vince had jumped into the back seat, Miles said sternly, "All right, Vince, we're going to let you in on what's going on—but you can't tell anybody, okay?"

"Of course," said Vince. "What do you think I am—an idiot?"

Miles raised his eyebrows but somehow resisted the temptation to answer the question. Instead, he told Vince all about their secret plan to crush the Diggers. The Winters were desperate to pay back Fox Swift and his friends for the humiliation of last year's Grand Final defeat.

The plan was simple: Miles had sneakily approached the parents of the best players from all the other teams in the district and offered them money in exchange for their son agreeing to play for the Dragons. Paying players was strictly against the competition rules, but Miles had always believed that if you don't get caught, then it's not really cheating.

Miles was confident that his new Dragons side would be the greatest junior football team ever assembled. He had already come up with a nickname for them: 'The Unbeatables'.

After Miles finished explaining his fiendish plan, Vince

sat in the back of the car with a thoughtful expression on his face.

"So what do you think, Vince?" asked Mace.

After a short pause, Vince responded, "I'll still be vice-captain, right?"

There was an awkward silence.

"Umm … is that a new T-shirt you're wearing, Vince?" said Mace, quickly changing the subject.

Fox and Lewis were up one end of the Swifts' backyard and Chase and Jimmy were down the other. As Fox casually kicked a long, accurate drop punt, he tried to remember the last time he had seen Chase or Jimmy fumble the footy.

He turned to Lewis and said, "With these two, it's kind of like the football is an obedient pet that does everything it's told."

Lewis smiled. "Cool—imagine what it would be like if your footy actually was a pet!"

He then started talking as if the football was a cute little puppy.

"Here, ball! Come on, fella! Come on! Bounce into my arms! There's a good ball … Now jump on to my foot. That's it … Now go through those two big sticks … That-a-ball!"

Lewis' hilarious "puppy-ball" commentary was

disturbed by the arrival of a real pet. Someone's pet rabbit had entered the backyard through a hole in the fence and was running around chasing after the football.

"Wow!" said Fox, who had never seen a creature so energetic. "He's nearly as fast as you, Lewis!"

"He's probably a better kick, too," joked Lewis' younger brother Jimmy.

Fox kicked the ball to his brother, Chase, and the snow-white rabbit immediately set off after it. Chase marked the ball and the rabbit started running around him in circles so fast that it became just a white blur as it went round and round and round. This made Chase laugh so hard he could barely stand up to kick the ball. He suggested they call the rabbit 'Gary' after the Gold Coast Suns superstar Gary Ablett, because it was so speedy and elusive.

An hour later the boys were still laughing uncontrollably at Gary's antics when Mrs Swift slid open the flywire door and came outside.

"Okay boys, that's enough mucking around," she said. "School starts tomorrow and Lewis and Jimmy need to get home."

"Awww, but Mum …" said Fox.

"And someone needs to finish tidying up their room!"

"Yeah, Fox!" teased Chase.

"I was referring to you, Chase!" said Mrs Swift.

"Awww, but Mum …" said Chase, making everyone laugh.

As Fox reluctantly went inside, he turned back to wave goodbye to Gary.

"I wonder whose rabbit that is," he thought.

"**M**ace, have you fed your rabbit?" asked Mrs Winter.

Mace didn't even look up from his Xbox game.

"*I'm* not going to feed the stupid rabbit!" he said.

"It's *your* rabbit!" said his mother.

"I never wanted a rabbit!" said Mace angrily.

"Yes, you did," said Mrs Winter. "You even threw a tantrum in the pet store when we said you couldn't have one."

This was true. Mace had caused a terrible scene in

the 'Paws 'n' Claws' pet store last year. About a week later, his father had evicted an elderly pensioner called Matilda Wall from her house because she hadn't paid him her rent. This wasn't really Matilda's fault, as she was in hospital in a coma at the time, but Miles had kicked her out anyway. Matilda had a beautiful snow-white rabbit that lived in a hutch in the backyard, and Miles had decided to take the rabbit and give it to Mace to calm him down after his dummy spit in the pet store.

"Well, I didn't know how lame rabbits were back then," said Mace. "Anyway, I'm way too busy to feed it."

Mrs Winter sighed as Mace went back to playing his video game, and went outside to feed the rabbit herself.

A minute later she rushed back inside in a panic.

"The rabbit has escaped!" she shrieked.

Mace didn't even look up from his game. "Who cares?" he said.

"Aren't you going to go and look for it?" asked Mrs Winter.

"Nah," said Mace. "It's probably been caught by a fox by now."

2

Playing Chasey

Fox bounced out of bed the next morning. He would never admit it, but he was really looking forward to going back to school and catching up with his friends. Chase was exactly the same. When Fox entered the kitchen, his brother was already there eating a large bowl of cereal.

Mr Swift was next to arrive. On seeing his sons already at the breakfast table, he put on a shocked expression, checked his watch and whistled.

"You boys must be *very* keen to get to school!" he said.

"No way, Dad—school is *so* lame," said Chase.

Mr Swift raised his eyebrows and winked at Fox.

"Okay then, Chase," he said. "You can stay at home today and I'll just drop off Fox."

"Huh?" said Chase.

"If you really think school is so lame, then you don't

have to go today."

"Um … You know, Dad … ahhh … I may as well go in," said Chase, with a hint of panic in his voice.

"No, no, I insist—you stay at home," said Mr Swift.

"Yeah, don't worry, Chase," said Fox, "I'll tell Jimmy, and I'm sure he'll find someone else to kick the footy with at lunchtime."

"But, but—" stammered Chase.

"No buts—my mind is made up," said Mr Swift.

At this point, Mrs Swift walked in and Chase blurted out, "Mum, Dad says I'm not allowed to go to school today!"

"Really?" said Mrs Swift, putting her hands on her hips and pretending to give her husband a stern look.

"It's against the law—I have to go, don't I?" pleaded Chase.

"You certainly do," replied his mother.

Chase looked very relieved and Mr Swift smiled at his wife.

"Oh, by the way, Dad, you don't have to give us a lift to school," said Fox. "We can just ride our bikes like we usually do."

"Nonsense, it's the first day of the school year— I always take you in on the first day."

"But you always do something really embarrassing!" said Chase.

"I'm not even going to get out of the van—how could

I possibly embarrass you?" asked Mr Swift innocently.

Fox and Chase exchanged a nervous glance. If anyone could embarrass them without leaving his car, it was their father.

Davinal Primary had expanded its classes this year because of school closures in the district, which meant that the principal, Mr Renton, had set up new portable classrooms to cater for Year 7 and Year 8 students in the area. This was partly made possible by a donation from Miles Winter. As always, Miles had insisted the school install a special plaque with his name on it. Unfortunately, at the unveiling of the plaque, it became apparent that the engraver had made another mistake. Last time the engraver had accidentally written: "This kind donation was made by Piles Winter." This time it was even worse. This time, the sign read: "These portables were built using the kind donation made by Slime Whiner."

Mr Swift drove his green Kombi van into the school car park and his sons leapt out.

"Maybe Dad really won't embarrass us this time," Fox thought hopefully.

Suddenly Miles Winter also drove into the car park, and pulled up next to the Kombi. As Mace and his younger twin brothers got out of the car, Miles leant over, wound down the passenger window and yelled to Fox's dad, "Hey Swift, when are you going to get rid of that green pile of junk you're driving?!"

Mr Swift revved his engine as if he was driving a racing car, and everyone in the vicinity turned and stared.

"Junk? What are you talking about, bro?" he said in a New Zealand accent. "This machine is fast as, bro ... Come on, bro—you want to dance, bro?"

"So much for Dad not embarrassing us!" Fox said to Chase.

Miles smiled. "Okay, Swift, I'll race you to the school gate. The winner gets to call the loser a 'loser'!"

Mr Swift revved his engine. Fox could not believe his dad was about to race his Kombi against Miles' sports car.

"On the count of three, Swift," yelled Miles over the din. "One, two ..."

Always a cheater, Miles sped off before he said "three".

Stones were flicked into the air as Miles' sports car lurched forward. Mr Swift, on the other hand, had taken off at an even slower speed than normal, making everyone who was watching crack up with laughter.

Miles looked into his rear-view mirror and smirked, "I showed you, Swift, you loser!"

Because he was looking in the mirror instead of watching where he was going, Miles failed to see the giant speed bump that was located just before the school gate. His car hit the bump going way too fast, soared upwards and, on landing, skidded into a small post, with a loud bang.

Miles made a mental note to write a nasty letter to the car manufacturer, because the safety air bag had failed to inflate. Luckily he was wearing his seatbelt and wasn't *physically* hurt, but his pride was going to be severely dented if he didn't win the race. The gate was less than 2 metres away and he frantically tried to restart his car before Mr Swift caught up. Alas, the car's engine refused to turn over, and as the Kombi van puttered slowly past, he saw Mr Swift make the letter 'L' on his forehead with his fingers, and mouth the word "Loser".

"Noooooooooooooooo!" screamed Miles.

In frustration he pounded his steering wheel really hard with his fists. Suddenly the air bag exploded out, pinning Miles to his seat.

"Oh, *now* the airbag works!" he shouted.

While waiting for his new teacher to appear in the classroom, Fox chatted excitedly to his Diggers teammates Lewis, Hugo, Paige, Simon and Bruno. Out of the corner of his eye he noticed a small, slightly built Asian boy he hadn't seen at school before.

Mace and Vince had noticed him as well and went over to "welcome" him to Davinal. They were armed with screwed-up balls of paper that were tightly bound together by masking tape.

Mace sneered and said, "Hey, Karate Kid, why don't you go back to Asia?!"

"Well, Mace, technically Australia *is* part of Asia. You know—*Australasia*," pointed out Vince.

Mace could not believe that the first fact Vince had ever remembered was one that made him look like a fool.

"Shut up, Vince!" he roared.

Before Fox could rush over to stop them, the two bullies were throwing their paper bombs at the defenceless new student. Fox could not believe what happened next.

With the reflexes of a cat, the boy used his hands to deflect both paper missiles into the air and then, as they came down, he snatched them out of the air and started juggling them.

"Thanks, guys—that was a fun game!" the boy said, smiling enthusiastically at Mace and Vince.

Everyone burst out laughing, which made Mace even angrier. He opened his mouth to respond, but was interrupted by a collective groan from the class. The new teacher had just walked through the door.

"No, it can't be!" thought Fox.

But it was. Their teacher this year was ... Mr Grinter.

"Unbelievable!" whispered Lewis. "It's like being struck by lightning—twice!"

Mr Grinter's fashion sense had not improved over the holidays. He was wearing a light-purple short-sleeved polo top, which appeared to be inside out. This was tucked into a pair of dark-green shorts that were hitched up around his rib cage. To top off the ensemble, Mr Grinter was wearing long white socks with his faded brown sandals.

Fox also noticed that Mr Grinter still had a problem with perspiration. The sweat stains under the arms of his polo top were a sight to behold.

"The stain under his left arm kind of looks like an angry octopus," whispered Lewis.

It really did, and when Lewis showed Fox his artistic interpretation of the stain, Fox had to pinch himself really hard so that he wouldn't fall down laughing.

As the students slowly took their seats, Mr Grinter apologised for being late.

"Sorry about that," he mumbled sheepishly. "I'm a teensy bit behind schedule because I, um … had to help an old lady cross the road. Old people, hey, what can you do?"

The blonde girl in the front of the class immediately started scribbling down a note.

"Ah, no need to write that down, Sally," the teacher said nervously.

Sally was the daughter of Principal Renton, and Mr Grinter was certain she took notes about his mistakes to show her dad after school each day.

"Okay, we are going to start off today with a bit of geography," he said in his droning voice.

The class let out another collective groan.

About five minutes later, as Fox was struggling to stay awake, Mr Grinter said, "… and the capital of Brazil, as we all know, is Rio de Janeiro …"

Two hands immediately shot up in the air. One of them was Hugo's, as usual. The other hand belonged to the new boy.

Mr Grinter had been embarrassed by Hugo correcting his mistakes many times before, so he ignored his hand and looked directly at his new student.

"Um, let's hear from you there, um …"

Mr Grinter checked a roll-call list on his desk, searching for the new boy's name.

"Ah, here it is," he said. "Hopefully I can pronounce this correctly: Ch-ung L-ee."

Mr Grinter then started speaking very slowly, as if Chung Lee was a two-year-old.

"Why. Are. You. Putting. Your. Hand. Up. Chung?"

he asked. "Do. You. Need. To. Visit. The. Toilet? You. Want. To. Go. Pee-pee?"

"No, sir," replied Chung, raising his eyebrows at Mr Grinter's crazy question. "You said Rio de Janeiro, but Brasilia is the capital of Brazil, and it has been since 1960."

"Are you sure about that?" said Mr Grinter, reaching for his atlas.

"It's definitely Brasilia," said Hugo.

"Well according to this atlas, the answer is ... um, Brasilia ... Ahhh, no need to write that down, Sally."

But it was too late. To Mr Grinter's dismay, Sally was shaking her head in disbelief as she jotted something down in her notebook.

As soon as the bell for recess was heard, Chung shot out the door of the classroom with Mace and Vince in hot pursuit. Fox and Lewis flew after them, wanting to make sure the new boy didn't get hurt.

But Fox soon discovered that Chung was full of surprises. Despite their best efforts, Mace and Vince could not catch him. Whenever the bullies got close, Chung would quickly change direction, completely wrong-footing them.

Chung was so elusive that neither boy managed to lay a finger on him. What infuriated Mace even more was that Chung kept saying, "Thanks for playing chasey with me! You guys are fun!"

As they ran past where Fox and Lewis were standing,

Chung doubled back and ran right in between Mace and Vince.

"Got you now, China Boy!" said Mace as he made a desperate lunge, but he completely missed Chung. Instead Mace went crashing straight into Vince, and the two bullies almost knocked each other out.

Fox and Lewis burst out laughing.

"Get lost, Swift," said Mace, slowly rising to his feet. "You and your Diggers mates are the biggest losers in the world."

"Losers?" asked Lewis. "Mmm … let me look that up in my dictionary."

Lewis proceeded to pull out an imaginary dictionary and flick through some imaginary pages.

"Ah yes, here it is. 'Losers: Losers are kids who play in winning premiership teams.' I guess we are losers. Hey, there's even a photo here of Hugo kicking the winning goal!"

"Really? What page is that on?" asked Vince.

"Shut up, Vince!" yelled Mace.

"Anyway, the Diggers are going to get wiped this year," boasted Vince. "We're going to be called 'The Unbeatables', because we've gone and re—"

"Vince!" screamed Mace.

As they started to walk off, Mace shook his head and said to Vince, "I am going to have to buy some tape and put it over your mouth!"

"Ooh, don't get the really sticky stuff—that really hurts when you rip it off," said Vince.

Fox was wondering what Vince had been about to say when he spotted his brother walking towards him.

"Hey, Chase," he said, "you will never be able to top this for bad news—my new teacher is Mr Grinter!"

"Oh yeah?" said Chase. "You think you've got problems. Your old footy coach Mr Percy is back in town—and he's *my* teacher!"

"What?!" said Fox and Lewis together.

Mr Percy had been sacked from his job at the Botanic Gardens in the city after he refused to help a pregnant lady with a pram down a flight of stairs. Not only had he refused her request for help, but he had also said to her, "It sucks to be you."

Unfortunately for Mr Percy, the husband of the pregnant lady had turned out to be the manager of the Botanic Gardens, and he had sacked Mr Percy on the spot.

"Who cares?" Mr Percy had said. "I'll just get a job at *another* Botanic Gardens in the city."

But sadly for Mr Percy, the city only had one Botanic Gardens, and he was forced to move back to Davinal. He really needed some money, so when he saw an advertisement for a teaching job at Davinal Primary, he applied for it straight away.

His job interview with the school's principal was going terribly until Mr Percy noticed a limp apple tree out the front of Mr Renton's office. Mr Renton explained he had been trying to grow some apples but nothing he did seemed to get the tree to bear fruit.

"I've even tried singing to that stupid tree," he'd confessed.

When Mr Percy assured the principal he had a special fertiliser that would not only make the apples grow but would make them grow BIG, Mr Renton's eyes had lit up, and he'd offered Mr Percy the teaching job immediately.

"Mr Percy is your teacher? Oh my God!" said Fox, who could not stop himself from laughing.

"Oh, you think that's funny, do you?" said Chase. "Well, the joke's on you, Fox, because apparently Mr Percy wants his old Diggers coaching job back."

Fox stopped laughing.

"You cannot be serious!" he cried.

At the dinner table that night, Chase was telling Fox and his parents all about his first day at school. Fox was always amazed at how funny Chase could be, even if he didn't know he was being funny.

"And you want to know what else Mr Percy is

going to do?" Chase asked the rest of his family. "He has promised to take us on an excursion to his 'Plant Cemetery', where he buries his dead vegetables. Mmm, can't wait for that one!"

Fox had taken a sip of milk just before Chase started to tell this story, and he laughed so hard white liquid started to rush out of his nose.

Chase then started talking about the new kids in his class.

"There's this really pale-skinned boy with dark hair and he wears sunglasses at lunchtime," he said. "Yep, he's definitely an emu."

"You mean an *emo*!" said Fox.

"Whatever," said Chase. "Oh, and of course there's the Winter twins, Magnus and Murdoch."

"What are they like?" asked Fox.

"Mmm, let's see. Shifty, annoying, they think they're better than everyone else—and that's just their good points!"

"Mace would be proud," said Fox, with a grin.

"And we've got this other new kid called Gregor, who's like a giant—and he does the *best* burps!"

"Good to see you're getting a quality education there, Chase," said Mr Swift.

"And there's this Japanese girl who can make really cool shapes out of pieces of paper," said Chase.

"Origami," said Mrs Swift.

"No, her name is Masumi," corrected Chase.

Fox slapped his hand on his forehead and laughed.

Mrs Swift turned to him and said, "Speaking of new kids, I bumped into a lovely lady called Mrs Lee at lunchtime. I hope you made her son Chung feel welcome today."

"Um, yeah … sure I did," said Fox unconvincingly.

Mrs Swift looked at him and raised her eyebrows.

"Okay, Mum, so I kind of focused on catching up with old friends," said Fox. "But I promise I'll have a really good talk to him tomorrow."

"That's if Mace and Vince don't get to him first!" he thought.

3

Puffed Out

When Fox entered the classroom the next morning, he saw that Mace and Vince had backed Chung into a corner.

"Prepare to die, Ching-Chong," said Mace.

"Umm, Mace, I'm pretty sure his name is Chung—"

"Shut up, Vince!" said Mace.

Fox dashed over and pushed in between Chung and the two bullies.

"Don't even think about it, Mace," said Fox, with a steely glare.

"Oh, like you could stop us, Swift," snarled Mace.

Fox smiled. "Maybe not on my own, but I'm pretty sure that with a little help from *these* guys, I could."

Mace and Vince spun around and saw Bruno, Simon and Paige standing behind them. Bruno and Simon were both tall, strong boys, but it was the angry look on Paige's face that scared Mace more than anything else.

"Okay, you win this round, Swift," he said. "But you can't protect that little China Boy forever."

"Don't worry about Mace," Fox said to Chung as Mace and Vince skulked back to their desks. "He hates *everyone*, especially me and the kids who play for the Diggers."

Before Fox could say anything else, Mr Grinter came through the door.

"Sorry I'm a little late," he said. "Umm … err … I had to pull a thorn out of a Labradoodle's paw."

Fox smiled as he looked across and saw Sally Renton furiously scribbling down a note.

At recess, Simon Phillips hung out with Chung, which discouraged Mace and Vince from continuing their vendetta against the new student.

Over by the oval, Fox was chatting with Paige, Hugo and Lewis when Bruno approached them.

Fox gave him a high five, as did Lewis and Paige, but Hugo suddenly pretended to do up his shoelace and left Bruno hanging.

The conversation that followed was fairly awkward, mainly because Hugo turned his back on his four friends and refused to speak. Fox was almost relieved when Bruno said, "See you guys in class."

"What was all that about, Hugo?" asked Paige

after Bruno had left. "Have you and Bruno had some sort of a fight?"

"I don't want to talk about it," said Hugo.

"Come on, bro—spill," said Lewis.

"Okay, okay!" said Hugo, throwing his hands in the air. "Bruno asked my sister to a movie. And I had to find out about it from my mum!"

None of the other three knew what to say. The uncomfortable silence was finally broken by Lewis, who said with a grin, "Jeez, if you get this worked up about a date, what'll you be like after their first *kiss*?!"

Fox tried to keep a straight face as Hugo's jaw dropped.

"That is *IT*, Lewis!" cried Hugo.

And with that, the slowest kid in school started chasing the fastest kid in school. While normally there was no way Hugo would ever catch his speedy friend, Lewis was laughing so hard he could hardly run.

Fox watched as the chase ended up on the school oval with Hugo making a desperate lunge and dragging Lewis to the ground.

As they rolled around on the oval, Lewis was still cracking up and Hugo was now smiling as well. They stopped wrestling and lay collapsed on the grass laughing and panting heavily.

Suddenly a serious expression came over Lewis' face. "Um, Hugo, we're on the grass …"

"Uh-oh," said Hugo.

Hugo was allergic to grass, and his arms, legs and face were already starting to swell up.

Fox and Paige ran over to help their friend, then supported him as they searched for a teacher.

Unfortunately the first teacher they bumped into was Mr Percy.

"Oh. My. God!" said Mr Percy, staring wide-eyed at Hugo. "You look like a Tetraodontidae!"

"A what?" said Fox.

"He means a puffer fish," explained Hugo—although because his tongue was now also slightly swollen, it came out as, "He meanth a puther fith."

"My point is," continued Mr Percy unsympathetically, "you look really, really ugly."

"Mr Percy, you're *really* not helping," said Paige. "Where should we take him? What should we do?"

"Maybe you should take him to the principal's office and ask to see the school medical officer?" said Mr Percy.

Fox and Lewis each put an arm around Hugo and helped him to walk. Fortunately, while Hugo was undoubtedly having a nasty allergic reaction to the grass, the swelling didn't seem to be getting any worse, and he was still breathing easily.

Fox was very surprised to see that Mr Percy was accompanying them to the principal's office.

"It's good of you to help," said Fox.

"Help?" said Mr Percy, looking confused. "I'm just going to check on the principal's apple tree."

As Mr Percy inspected Mr Renton's seven giant, shiny apples, Fox, Lewis and Paige assisted Hugo through a set of double doors, along a corridor and into the principal's waiting room.

Fox couldn't see anyone, but he could hear a faint scratching sound.

His eyes moved to where the sound was coming from and eventually he realised he was looking at the principal's assistant, Miss Carey. She was especially hard to see because the colour of her dress and her shoes matched the colour of the office walls almost exactly.

"She looks like a chameleon wearing glasses!" whispered Lewis.

Fox was even more astonished to notice that Miss Carey appeared to be scrubbing the wall with a toothbrush.

Miss Carey looked at the students. "Just smoothing out the wall," she explained casually.

"Nothing weird about that!" said Lewis out of the corner of his mouth.

"What did you say?" demanded Miss Carey.

"He said we need to see the medical officer straight away," cut in Fox, thinking quickly.

"Well, you're looking at her," said Miss Carey.

"*You're* the medical officer?" Fox said doubtfully.

"Mr Renton is cutting back on costs," explained Miss Carey.

"Well, what are you going to do about Hugo?" demanded Paige.

Miss Carey looked at Hugo for the first time, then shrieked and fled behind her desk. "What is *that*?" she cried.

Looking at Hugo, Fox could sort of understand Miss Carey's reaction. Hugo's face was so puffed up he could barely open his eyes, and his skin was a light shade of purple.

"What are you going to do to help Hugo?" said Paige.

Miss Carey opened a drawer in her desk, took out a small bandage and cautiously offered it to Hugo.

"Obviously you'll have to put it on yourself," she said.

Hugo took the bandage and studied it.

"Whath am I thoposed ta doo with tha bandath?" he said.

Miss Carey didn't reply, as she was too busy applying anti-germ cream to her hands. She then took out a pristine white handkerchief and tied it over her mouth.

"He doesn't have leprosy!" cried Lewis in frustration.

"Pleath call my mutha," said Hugo.

Miss Carey rolled her eyes as if she were being asked to do a gigantic favour, then looked up the Trippitts' emergency contact phone number on the computer and rang Hugo's mother.

"Hello Mrs Trippitt? … Yes, it's Miss Carey—what? … Someone already called you on the mobile? … What does Hugo look like? Mmm … did you ever see that film called *The Elephant Man*? … Ooh, the phone dropped out."

While they waited for Mrs Trippitt to arrive, Lewis cheered Hugo up by giving him a cool new nickname, 'Puff Trippitt', and then performing a special rap song in Puff's honour.

Lewis started off by making a drumbeat sound—"Pa poom poom poom, pa poom poom poom"—and then launched into a rap that he made up on the spot:

His name is Puff-dog Trippitt
He's got brain cells by da mill-i-on
But when he rolls on grass
He's like a balloon all filled with hel-i-um!

This was when Fox noticed Miss Carey do something he had never seen her do before: smile. But when she realised Fox was looking, Miss Carey's normal grumpy face returned.

Lewis nodded to Fox and Paige to provide him with a beat. They responded with "Pa poom poom poom, pa poom poom poom …" and Lewis continued with his rap:

He's like Popeye da sailor

After he eats all dat spinach
They both got great big muscles
I swear Hugo's da mirror image!

Fox was amazed and impressed that Lewis had managed to rhyme "spinach" with "image".

In last year's Grand Final
Puffy kicked the winning goal
The Diggers crowd went crazy
And it destroyed Mace Winter's soul!

Fox was pretty sure that Hugo would be smiling from ear to ear after hearing this verse, but it was impossible to tell because his face was so swollen.

When Puff-dog drinks his soy milk
There ain't no way he'd just sip it
Yeah he slurps it through his nose
'Coz he's a wild one that Puff Trippitt.

Fox looked over and was blown away to see Miss Carey joining in with the, "Pa poom poom poom, pa poom poom poom ..."

Puff Trippitt you da man
But next time avoid da grass
'Coz every part of you swells up
'Specially your big fat a—

Right at this moment Mrs Trippitt entered the room, causing Lewis to change the last word of his rap.

"—a ... ankles," he stammered, blushing slightly.

Hugo's mum rushed over to her son, gave him a huge hug then handed him an anti-inflammatory tablet and a bottle of water to wash it down.

"That should help the swelling for now," she said warmly, "but let's get you to the doctor."

Fox shook Hugo's hand, Paige gave him a hug and Lewis gave him a special 'Puff Trippitt' drawing.

"Hey Mum," said Hugo. "Who called you to let you know I wath thick?"

"Bruno did, dear," said Mrs Trippitt.

"Bruno? Aw thath nithe," said Hugo, suddenly regretting he'd been so frosty towards his friend.

But just before they walked out the door Hugo stopped and said, "Hang on, Mum, how come Bruno hath your mobile number?!"

Paige, Lewis and Fox looked at each other and burst out laughing.

ox was surprised to see Hugo back at school the next morning, but as Lewis pointed out, "Hugo missing school is like you missing a football game."

Hugo's eyes were still a little puffy, but his normal skin colour had returned and he smiled when Lewis referred to him as 'Puffy-D'.

To everyone's surprise, Mr Grinter actually managed to arrive at class on time, which sent all the students scurrying to their desks.

"Here I am, punctual as always," he said briskly.

He then nodded at Sally in the front row, hoping she would make a note about his timely arrival. Unfortunately for Mr Grinter, Sally simply put down her pen, folded her arms and stared back at him.

"Okay," said Mr Grinter, "this morning we will be focusing on maths …"

The class let out a long, loud groan.

"Now, now," said Mr Grinter, "maths might seem hard but you can always improve—even Albert Einstein once failed mathematics …"

Two hands immediately shot up in the air—they belonged to Chung and Hugo.

Speaking extremely slowly, Mr Grinter said, "Chung. Do. You. Want. To. Know. Who. Albert. Einstein. Is?"

"No, thank you," replied Chung in faultless English, "I know who Albert Einstein was—he was a brilliant theoretical physicist who lived between 1879 and 1955. He developed the theory of general relativity and—"

"Yes, we all know that," snapped Mr Grinter, who really didn't have a clue. "Why. Did. You. Put. Up. Your. Hand?"

"Because you said he failed mathematics," said Chung. "That's incorrect—in fact by the age of 15, Einstein had mastered differential and integral calculus. The only exam he is known to have failed was an entrance exam to the Swiss Federal Polytechnic School, but he was years younger than the other students at the time—and even in that exam he did brilliantly in the maths and science sections."

Mr Grinter was completely gobsmacked, as was the rest of the class. The only sound that could be heard was Sally Renton's pen, as she started scribbling something down in her notebook.

At recess Fox cautiously asked Hugo, "Do you think Chung might be as smart as you?"

"Maybe," said Hugo.

"Well, why don't you find out by telling him one of your smart jokes?" said Lewis.

"Huh? My *fart* jokes?" said Hugo.

"No, *smart* jokes, said Lewis. "You know, those jokes you tell that none of us get, but you crack yourself up laughing? Although for the record I do think fart jokes are pretty funny."

"Good call—if Chung laughs at one of Hugo's jokes, then he must be brilliant, too!" said Fox.

Hugo agreed to give it a try, and called Chung over. "Hey, I've got a joke for you," he said. "A photon is going through airport security, right? And the customs officer asks if he has any luggage. And the photon says, 'No, I'm travelling *light*!'"

Chung immediately laughed hysterically, while Fox, Lewis and Paige just stared at the two geniuses.

Chung then said to Hugo, "Hey, I've got one for you: what does a dyslexic, agnostic insomniac do at night? He stays up wondering if there really is a *dog*!"

Hugo laughed so hard he nearly choked, and he had to wipe away the tears that were flowing from his puffy eyes.

"My dad is a priest!" he said. "He's going to love that one—a *dog*! Classic!"

Fox didn't get the joke at all, but he laughed politely and said, "So Chung, umm ... What's your story?"

Chung explained that his dad had been a nuclear physicist in China until a few years ago, when his family had come out to Australia for a holiday, fell in love with the lifestyle and decided to move "down under". After settling in Melbourne, the family became Australian citizens a year later on Australia Day, a week before school started. Chung's dad, who had always lived in smog-filled, crowded cities, had decided to move to the countryside.

That's how Chung had ended up in Davinal.

"What sort of jobs are there for a nuclear physicist in Davinal?" asked Hugo.

"None ... Dad didn't really think that one through," joked Chung. "He's kind of weighing up his options at the moment."

After asking a few more questions, Fox discovered that Chung liked to do magic tricks.

"Could you show us one?" Fox asked eagerly.

Chung started to do some tricks, and very soon a small crowd had gathered to watch, which attracted the attention of Mace and Vince.

Coming over to investigate, Mace pushed his way to the front of the group and was put out to discover that Chung was the centre of attention.

"Magic is *so* lame!" said Mace in a loud voice. "It's always easy to spot the trick."

"Is it?" said Chung. "So Mace, what do you have in your top pocket?"

"That's easy," replied Mace. "I don't have anything in my top pocket."

"Are you *sure* about that, Mace?" asked Chung.

Vince, who was standing next to Mace, looked at his friend and said suddenly, "Yes you do, Mace!"

He then grabbed the heart-shaped piece of cardboard sticking out of his friend's pocket.

"It's a cardboard heart!" he announced excitedly.

"On one side it says, 'I love Fox' and on the other it says, 'I love the Diggers'."

Everyone laughed and Mace went bright red.

"Hey Mace," said a confused Vince, "why would you write that sort of stuff?! I thought you hated the Diggers?"

"I didn't write it, you idiot!" exploded Mace. "Give me that!"

Mace snatched the cardboard heart from Vince, ripped it into small pieces and threw the pieces into the air.

"That's what I think of your stupid magic, China Boy!" said Mace, before turning to storm off.

But Chung called after him, "Hey Mace, is there something *else* in your pocket?"

"There is nothing in my stupid pocket!" Mace said defiantly.

Chung raised his eyebrows. "Are you *sure* about that, Mace?" he said again.

Quickly sticking his hand in Mace's pocket, Vince pulled out another cardboard heart. On one side it said, "I REALLY love Fox" and on the other it said, "I REALLY love the Diggers".

"Wow!" exclaimed Vince. "That is amazing!"

"No it's not!" said Mace.

"Yeah, I mean ... no it's not," said Vince. "It is *so* obvious how you did that cardboard heart thing ...

umm, tell him how he did it, Mace."

"Well, it's, umm, he just kind of ... well ... you are *so* dead, Chung!"

With that, Mace went to grab the young magician, but Chung was too quick and slipped away easily.

"Looks like it's time for another game of chasey!" said Chung as he ran off with Mace and Vince in hot pursuit. Fox and his friends laughed, as time and time again Chung escaped from the clutches of the bullies.

As Chung ran by just before the bell went, Fox yelled out, "Hey, do you want to come around to my place after school?"

"Sure!" said Chung as he sprinted off towards the oval.

"I'll give you my address in class!" Fox called out after him.

"I think the Diggers might have found a new recruit," thought Fox, with a huge grin on his face.

4

Bouncing Back

Fox had never seen anyone dodge and sidestep like Chung Lee. He would start to move to the left, then in a flash he'd spin away to the right. He could bend, twist, turn and even do the splits.

"I'm pretty sure Chung is made of rubber," Lewis had commented as the three of them watched Chung skilfully evading Mace and Vince.

Fox had a theory that if Chung had the footy in a game, no opposition player would be able to catch him to tackle him. So if Chung could learn how to bounce the ball, he could keep running down the field towards the goals.

"And once he's mastered bouncing the ball, then all we need to do is teach him how to kick and handball," Fox said to Lewis, Paige and Hugo.

Fox's friends were sceptical, especially after Chung told them the only footy he had seen was during the sports reports on the TV news, but they agreed to meet at the Swifts' house after school for a special training session. Fox couldn't wait.

Just before his friends arrived, Mrs Swift came home and asked Fox how Chung was settling in at school.

"I think he's been having a bit of a rough time," replied Fox. "Anyway, I've asked him to come around this arvo."

"That's very kind of you, Fox," said Mrs Swift.

"Yeah, Fox thinks Chung could be a really good footballer for the Diggers," said Chase, "so he's going to test out his skills in the backyard."

Mrs Swift put her hands on her hips.

"So Fox, did you invite Chung around because you wanted to help him fit in at school, or because he is a potential football recruit?"

"Um ..."

Fortunately Fox was saved from answering the question by the sound of the doorbell.

"Better go and see who that is," he said as he set off down the corridor.

A few minutes later, Fox, Chase, Paige, Lewis, Hugo and Chung were all assembled in the backyard.

"Because of its shape, bouncing a footy is extremely difficult," explained Hugo, holding up a ball. "I've been playing Aussie Rules all my life and I still can't do it properly."

Chung looked a little overawed. "Sounds pretty complicated," he said, with a bewildered look on his face.

"Don't worry, Chung," said Fox. "I emailed Cyril Rioli and asked him to send through some tips—I'll see if he's replied."

Fox dashed inside the house and checked his parents' computer.

"Yes!" he cried.

Not only had Cyril replied, he had also sent through some diagrams showing how to bounce the ball, with added instructions like, "Keep your eye on the ball" and, "The end of the ball has to hit the ground to make it bounce back". Fox printed them off and looked at them closely.

The more Fox looked at the drawings, the more he began to doubt his plan.

"Hugo was right," he thought to himself. "Bouncing the ball really is a difficult skill. Just because I find it easy, I shouldn't expect others to ..."

Fox trailed off mid-thought when he looked up and out through the glass sliding doors into the backyard. He could not believe what he was seeing. Chung had two footballs and was running all over the place bouncing one with each hand!

"No way!" Fox said out loud. "That is ridiculous!"

Fox had trained himself to bounce one footy with either hand, but to bounce two at the same time while running flat out was incredible!

BOUNCING THE BALL

How to bounce the football:

Ⓐ Starting at a walk, bounce the ball with one hand slightly on top of the ball and push it down.

Ⓑ Fully extend your arm as you push the ball to the ground, bouncing the ball far enough in front so that it rebounds into your arms without altering your stride.

The ball should hit the ground on its front end at about 45 degrees and rotate forward as it rebounds towards your hands. Watch the ball closely throughout the bounce.

Ⓒ Watch the ball all the way back into your hand, using both hands to take it at mid-torso height.

When you feel comfortable at a walk, proceed to a jog, and then to full pace.

He headed outside and saw Chase staring at Chung with his mouth hanging open.

Chase turned to his brother and said, "You have *definitely* found a new recruit for the Diggers!"

"If he doesn't join the Diggers he should definitely join the circus!" declared Lewis.

What made the skilful exhibition even more of a spectacle was the reappearance of Gary the rabbit, who ran around with Chung as if they were teammates.

Chung walked over to Fox with Gary trailing behind him.

"That is the world's coolest rabbit," he said.

Fox then asked Chung if he would play for the Diggers, and explained why he thought he would be a star footballer.

"No one will be able to tackle you—you could be our **rover!**"

"Wow, a *Rover*!" said Chung, thinking Fox was referring to the robot that scientists had put on Mars to find out more about the planet. "Cool!"

"The next step for you is to practise bouncing the ball when people are trying to tackle you," said Paige.

Fox noticed that Hugo had put his fingers on his temples and was slowly moving them in small circles.

"I think I have an idea ..." he said.

In class the next day, Mr Grinter had his back to the students as he wrote some maths problems on the whiteboard. Mace, who had let his eyes wander around the room, looked over at Chung and was surprised to see he was holding a football. Then he realised it was *his* football! It was easy to tell it was his, because it had his name written on it in texta:

Mace's hand shot up in the air.

"Mr Grinter! Mr Grinter! The stupid new kid stole my footy!"

Mr Grinter spun around and looked at Chung, who was sitting innocently at his desk.

As usual, he spoke to Chung in an annoyingly slow manner.

"In. This. Country. Stealing. Bad. Mace. Say. You. Steal. His. Foot. Ball."

Chung looked at his accuser and said, "Are you quite sure about that, Mace? I'm certain I saw you put it into your bag this morning."

"Of course I'm sure, you slippery little thief!" said Mace. "It's not there, Mr Grinter! I'll show you …"

With that, Mace unzipped his bag—and stopped short. His footy was there all right, just where he'd left it. "But, but …" he stammered, "I swear I saw Chung …"

"Let's get back to work, shall we?" said Mr Grinter, returning his attention to the whiteboard.

Mace looked over at Chung and his eyes nearly popped out of his head—Chung had his football again. This time he was spinning it on his index finger as if it were a basketball.

In a flash, Mace's hand was back in the air and he cleared his throat to grab the attention of Mr Grinter, who turned around immediately. Mace was just about to report the theft of his footy for a second time when, throwing a dirty look in Chung's direction, he noticed the new student was now sitting innocently at his desk. The football was nowhere in sight.

"Yes, Mace?" said Mr Grinter.

"Um, nothing," replied Mace. "I was just stretching."

Mr Grinter wanted to give Mace a detention for being a pest, but he was too afraid of Mr Winter, so he just sighed and turned back to the whiteboard.

Mace's face was flushed with anger. He pointed at Chung, then pounded his fist into his hand and mouthed, "You. Are. So. Dead!"

He turned to Vince and whispered, "You know what we're going to do to Chung, don't you?"

"You bet," said Vince. "We're going ask him how he does that disappearing football trick—that is *sooo* cool!"

"Shut up, Vince!"

When the bell sounded for morning tea, Chung once again had Mace's footy in his hands.

"Lose something, Mace?" he asked before bolting out the door. Mace and Vince went flying after him, with Fox and his friends not far behind.

Fox watched as Mace and Vince tried to grab Chung, who easily dodged past them—and this time he was bouncing the ball as he did so.

"Great plan, Hugo," yelled Chung as he ran by his new Diggers friends. "This is the best bouncing practice ever!"

Chung was a complete natural at avoiding being tackled, but Fox made a mental note to ask Cyril for some extra tips on how to **baulk** and dodge around players.

By the time the bell went to signal a return to class, Mace and Vince were completely exhausted. Their shirts were hanging out, they were dripping with sweat, and their knees were covered in dirt. Chung, on the other hand, looked as fresh as he had at the start of the day.

"We didn't get you today, Chung, but we *will* get you," promised Mace as Chung bounced the football past where the bullies lay panting on the ground.

"Yeah, you can't keep running forever," said Vince.

Fox knew that Mace and Vince were right. They would never give up trying to catch Chung. Unless …

Fox, pretending to be Hugo, put his fingers on his temples and slowly moved them around in small circles.

"I think I might have an idea …"

Just before the lunchtime bell, Fox turned to Lewis and whispered rather loudly, "I've got a secret I want to tell you outside."

Vince's desk was nearby, and his ears pricked up immediately. He looked the other way, pretending not to listen.

"Excellent! Who's the secret about?" asked Lewis.

"It's about Chung, but you can't tell anyone."

"No worries—let's meet near the water fountain."

Vince could not believe his luck. He was determined to find out about Chung's secret and report back to Mace. So as soon as Mr Grinter said they could go, he bolted out the door and ran to the water fountain. He pressed a small silver button that sent a stream of water into his mouth and thought, "Now all I have to do is wait."

Sure enough, Fox and Lewis arrived shortly afterwards and stood about a metre away from the water fountain. Vince kept slurping down water so that Fox wouldn't think he was spying.

"So what's this secret about Chung?" asked Lewis.

"It's amazing," said Fox. "Chung is actually a martial arts champion!"

Vince made a loud, nervous gulping sound, which the other two boys pretended not to hear.

"No way!" said Lewis. "So you're telling me Chung knows all those lethal kung fu moves?"

Lewis then started doing a series of karate chops and kicks in the air.

"Yikes!" thought Vince. "What's Mace going to think when I tell him Chung has a deadly karate chop?"

"Yep, he's a black belt. And best of all he knows this special grip that— No, I'd better not say."

"Come on, Fox, you gotta tell me!" pleaded Lewis.

"Yeah, come on, Fox, tell him!" thought Vince, who had by now slurped down nearly 2 litres of water.

"You can't tell anyone!"

"You got it, Fox. Come on—spill!" Lewis said excitedly.

"Okay. Chung has this special martial arts move called 'The P.O.D Grip'," said Fox.

"The P.O.D. Grip?" asked Lewis.

"It stands for 'Pee On Demand'. All Chung has to do is touch you with two fingers on a certain part of your shoulder, and *bam!* You instantly wet your pants!"

"Get out of here! You wet your pants?"

"And he's planning to use it on Mace and Vince if they ever catch him. Imagine if those two wet their pants in front of everyone at school ..."

Vince had heard enough. Besides, with the huge amount of water he had just consumed, all this talk about peeing meant he was busting to go to the toilet. He stopped drinking and shuffled off, to the delight of the seven kids who were waiting in the water fountain queue behind him.

Just before afternoon classes started, Vince sprinted up to Mace to pass on the news.

"Mace, you won't never believe what I'm gonna tell ya," he said.

"You passed an English test?" asked Mace sarcastically.

Not realising he had just been insulted, Vince said, "No, it's about Chung."

"Good," said Mace, "because I've got a plan on how we can grab him after school."

"No!" said Vince urgently. "That's what he wants! He's a kung fu master and when we grab him he's going to give us the P.O.D. Grip!"

"The P.O.D. Grip?" said Mace, raising his eyebrows.
Vince rolled his eyes.

"I thought *everyone* knew what that was!" he said,
trying to act like he was an expert on martial arts.

Mace didn't want to admit to Vince that he was
clueless so he said, "Yeah, of course I know what it is
… um, just remind me again."

Vince was one of those people who is always happy to
make up answers whenever they don't have all the facts.

"The P.O.D. is this ancient Chinese grip, where Chung
gets his hand like this," explained Vince, making a claw
with his own hand, "and he kind of spins around like
this and makes this 'Howaaaaah!' sort of sound. Then
he strikes you on the shoulder like a cobra snake, and he
hits some special nerve that makes you wet your pants!"

Mace's eyes widened. "Chung can make us wet
our pants?"

"Yep, in front of the whole school—that's his plan to
make us look stupid."

"Well, we're not going to fall for that," said Mace.
"No more chasing Chung."

When they sat down in class, Vince pulled out two
square sheets of plastic that he normally used to cover
his books, and put one under his bottom. He offered
the other one to Mace.

"What's that for?" asked Mace.

"In case Chung gets us with the P.O.D. Grip in class."

"Shut up, Vince!" said Mace.

Mace looked over and saw Chung sitting down at his desk doing what appeared to be kung fu moves with his hands. Chung turned, stared Mace straight in the eyes, and made a claw with his right hand.

Mace snatched the plastic sheet from Vince and shoved it under his bottom.

5

Junk (Food) Mail

Mr Scott sat on the worn-out brown couch in his lounge room, flipping through one of his old footy scrapbooks. The Diggers' coach had been a brilliant young footballer—so good, in fact, that the Hawthorn Football Club had recruited him when he was only 17 years old. And then he'd hurt his knee.

He stared at the headline of the faded newspaper clipping in front of him: '13 Goals—An Unlucky Number For **Bush Star!**'

He started to read the article underneath.

Greg Scott, Hawthorn's gun recruit from Davinal, kicked 13 goals before three-quarter time in yesterday's final practice match. In the final quarter, after taking a spectacular mark, Scott

landed heavily on his left knee and had to be
stretchered off. Hawks fans will be hoping it is
not a serious injury, as this kid has all the makings
of a superstar ...

Unfortunately the injury *was* serious, and Greg Scott
was told he would never play football again. He took
the news badly, turning his back on the outside world
and choosing to be alone with his memories and dreams
of what might have been. Over the next 40 years he
rarely left his house, but that had all changed the day
Fox Swift had knocked on his door and asked him to
coach the Davinal Diggers ...

Mr Scott's thoughts were interrupted by a knock at
the door.

"Spooky," he thought.

He went to the front door and peered through the
peephole. Standing on his doorstep was a plump,
balding man with a pencil-thin moustache, wearing a
safari suit. His face looked vaguely familiar, but Mr
Scott couldn't work out where he had seen him before.

He opened the door and said, "Hello, can I help you?"

"Hi Gregory," said Safari Suit, "it's so nice to meet
you in person. I'm Mr Percy—ta-da!"

Mr Percy waved both of his arms in the air as he said
"ta-da" as if to say, "I know you must have heard about
me—and now here I am! Aren't you lucky?!"

"Umm ... I'm not really sure who ... wait a minute—

were you the coach of the Diggers before I took over?"

"Bingo!" said Mr Percy with an unusual amount of charm. "And I just want to say what a wonderful job you did as *caretaker* coach while I was away."

"Caretaker coach?" said Mr Scott, folding his arms.

"That's right, but I'm back now—obviously, because I'm standing right in front of you, ha—so I'll be taking back the coaching position now."

Mr Percy hated football, but he wanted to coach the Diggers again so he could say he supported the local community in any upcoming job interviews. He loathed living in Davinal—a place he described as a "cultural desert"—and was desperate to move back to the city.

"Anyhoo," continued Mr Percy, "just thought I'd let you know so you didn't bother turning up to training this year ..."

At this point Mr Percy sensed a presence behind him. He slowly turned around—and found himself face-to-face with a kangaroo.

"Eeek!"

"I don't think Joey likes you very much, Mr Percy," said Mr Scott. "And she's normally a pretty good judge of character."

"Umm ... Mr Scott, I think we may have started out on the wrong foot," stammered Mr Percy, eyeing off the hostile kangaroo. "How about you and I go inside and have a nice chat about this over a cup of tea?"

"There is nothing to chat about. I'll be coaching the Diggers this year—end of story."

"Okay, okay. I hear what you're saying," said Mr Percy. "How about I let you be my assistant coach?"

"I don't think so."

"How about we go rock, paper, scissors?"

"No."

"Best of three?"

"Please leave, Mr Percy."

"You can't make me!"

"Maybe *I* can't, but—" And with that, Mr Scott stepped inside and slammed the door, leaving Mr Percy to deal with a rather angry kangaroo.

Joey only moved forward a couple of centimetres, but this was more than enough to cause Mr Percy to run screaming down the footpath. He jumped into his car and locked all the doors, and sat there stewing.

"I know what I'll do," he thought. "I'll take back all my giant vegetables that the Diggers use at training. That'll show them!"

Just as he was realising he didn't have any space to store the oversized vegetables in his tiny one-room flat, he looked up and saw Joey staring at him through the passenger window of his car.

"Bad luck, you dumb marsupial—you can't get me in here!" taunted Mr Percy. "Nah, nah, na-nah-nah!"

But as Joey's paw moved towards the car's door

handle, Mr Percy's face went white with fear.

"Oh my God, it's trying to break into my car!" he cried and quickly started his engine.

As Mr Percy sped off down the street with Joey hopping after him, Mr Scott, who had been watching from his front window, burst out laughing.

Mace was certain the Dragons would beat the Diggers this season. With his dad secretly paying and recruiting the best footballers in the district, how could they lose? But he didn't want to take any chances.

He was determined to come up with a plan to stop the Diggers' star full-forward, Simon Phillips, from kicking goals. At the start of last year, Simon had been extremely overweight. He used to hide lollies in his footy socks, and Mace had even heard a rumour he took cream buns with him to eat in the shower!

Then, all of a sudden, Simon had stopped

eating junk food and started training hard. He lost all his excess weight and became a star goalkicker for the Diggers.

"I have to make him start eating junk food again," thought Mace.

Mace's scheme was simple: he bought lots of different chocolate bars, put them in a box, and posted them to Simon.

The day the chocolate bars were due to arrive, Mace hid in the bushes near Simon's place and waited. He watched as Simon took the package from the mailbox, shook it, then ripped it open. On seeing the contents, Simon's eyes lit up and he raced inside his house.

"Excellent," thought Mace, "he'll be fatter than a hippopotamus in no time."

Every day for the next month Mace posted large bundles of chocolate bars to Simon, and every day Simon would smile and run inside with his package.

"Looks like the Diggers are about to have a very *full* forward," thought Mace, with a smug grin.

Fox and Chase rode their bikes around to the old Davinal hospital that was now used as accommodation for refugee families. These families lived in the hospital while the Australian government made a decision on whether they would be allowed to stay down under or would have to return to where they had come from.

The Swift boys came here at least once a week to visit Sammy and Chris, the boys from Sudan. Fox had given them an old footy when they first met, and they had quickly become two of the Davinal Diggers' best players.

Fox had also noticed that since they started playing footy and hanging out with the Diggers players, their English had improved considerably.

As always, Sammy and Chris were waiting for them in the foyer just inside the entrance.

"Oh my God, they're even taller," whispered Chase.

"You say that every week," whispered Fox.

Fox had to agree with Chase, though—the boys did appear taller every time he saw them. They were giants—friendly giants with beaming smiles and wicked senses of humour.

"Heeeey," said Sammy, greeting Fox and Chase, "you want to play with dolls?"

Fox didn't know what to say. He looked at Chase, who was also speechless.

"We trick you!" said Chris. "Let's go kick footy."

Sammy was rolling around on the floor laughing.

"We trick you good! Dolls—ha!"

"Umm, I knew you guys were joking," said Fox. "I was just playing along."

"Me too," said Chase, feeling incredibly relieved.

Fox loved playing kick-to-kick with Sammy and Chris. They were not only tall, but also incredibly athletic. He still could not believe how quickly they had picked up AFL football.

"We show you something," said Sammy, signalling for Fox to lob up a kick.

Fox did as he was instructed. He kicked the ball high into the air and watched Chris stand under **the Sherrin** as it came down to earth.

Chris bent his back slightly, allowing Sammy to use him as a stepladder and soar into the air to take a **mark** metres above the ground.

Chase turned to Fox and said, "Look up in the sky— it's a bird! It's a plane! No, it's Super Sammy!"

"My turn!" said Chris.

This time Chase kicked the ball into the air and Sammy stood under it. Chris leapt up and pushed off Sammy's shoulder—and he too soared skyward and plucked the ball out of the air.

Fox had taken plenty of hangers in his time, but had never seen anyone fly as high as the two Sudanese boys.

"These guys are going to be amazing this season!" he thought.

Fox called them over and suggested they do a quick training drill Cyril Rioli called "Hot Spuds". The four of them formed a tight square and pretended that the footy was a hot potato that couldn't be held for longer than a split second. Whoever had the ball fired off handballs to anyone they liked, as quickly as they could. Fox liked this drill because you never knew when the ball was coming your way, so you had to stay alert. It was a great way to practise safe and sure hands under pressure.

After they got into a routine Fox called out, "Okay, from now on you're not allowed to handball back to whoever handballed it to you!" This made the drill more difficult as the boys needed to concentrate really hard, but the ball didn't hit the ground once!

After about 10 minutes they stopped for a break, and Chase asked Sammy and Chris the same question he asked them every week: "Who is your favourite AFL player?"

Every week they gave the same answer: "Nic Nat!"

Nic Naitanui was a star West Coast player. He was fast and mobile, and took spectacular marks. And his parents had also moved from overseas—Fiji.

Fox remembered the first time Sammy and Chris had seen Nic Nat play on television. They'd suddenly stood up, pointed at the screen and started clapping. And, when Nic Nat had taken a huge mark seconds later, they'd both jumped to their feet and started dancing!

Now, when people asked Sammy and Chris what they wanted to do when they were older, they simply said

"Nic Nat". Having just seen a few of their high-leaping marks, Fox had no doubt they would achieve their goal of playing in the big League. He started to daydream about how cool it would be if one day Sammy, Chris, Chase and he all played together on **the MCG** ...

"Hey, isn't that Simon?" asked Chase, interrupting his brother's daydream.

Fox looked over and saw Simon Phillips pushing a small trolley out the back door of the old hospital building. He was being followed by about 30 of the kids from the centre, who were all laughing and smiling. He waved to Fox and continued on around to the side of the hospital.

"What's going on?" asked Fox.

"Simon always come here," said Chris.

"Everybody love Simon," said Sammy with a smile.

"He train the kids to exercise," explained Chris.

"Come see," said Sammy.

The four of them went over to where Simon was standing in front of the kids, who were spread out on a large section of grass. The children were all chatting and mucking around, but as soon as Simon started to talk, they stopped and gave him their full attention.

"Okay everyone, follow me, starting with jogging on the spot ... That's it, lifting up those knees ... Now drop down for five push-ups ... Quick, back up and jogging on the spot again ... Now five star jumps ..."

Fox was exhausted just watching all the activity, but the kids were absolutely loving the training session. They were smiling and laughing as they tried to keep up with Simon.

After a solid 30-minute workout, Simon congratulated all the kids for putting in a great effort. Then he walked over to his trolley and said, "Okay, who wants a treat?"

All the kids put their hands in the air and jumped around.

"Everyone gets a piece of fruit and a chocolate bar," said Simon, "but what's the rule?"

"Eat the fruit first!" yelled out all the kids.

And with that Simon started distributing small packages to the young refugees. When he had finished, Fox went over to Simon and gave him a friendly knuckle-punch.

"It is so cool what you're doing," said Fox.

"It's nothing," said Simon modestly. "Someone keeps sending me chocolate bars—I don't want them, and I thought the odd bit of chocky wouldn't hurt these guys, especially if they are exercising and eating some fruit as well."

Fox was very proud of his friend, but as he rode home with Chase he wondered who could possibly be sending so much chocolate to Simon.

"Mace!" he cried, suddenly slamming on the brakes.

"Where?" asked Chase, immediately stopping his

bike and looking around nervously.

"No, I mean it could be Mace sending the chocolate bars to Simon—he wants Simon to eat them and get fat again!"

Chase started laughing and said, "But instead Simon gives away all the chocolate to the refugees!"

"That is hilarious," said Fox.

"To everyone except for Mace!" said Chase as he high-fived his brother.

6

Stand Up,
Fall Down

The students made their way into the assembly hall with all the enthusiasm of a visit to the dentist.

"Hugo, are you sure time doesn't go slower in first term?" asked Fox.

"Positive," said Hugo. "You just want time to go faster so the footy season can start."

Fox took a seat in the hall and looked across to where Mace and Vince were mucking around at the end of the row. Mace stared back at Fox, then tilted his head back slightly and gave an arrogant smirk.

"Mace is definitely up to something," said Fox. "He's been *really* cocky lately—even by his standards."

Mr Renton entered briskly from the back of the assembly hall, followed by a gaggle of teachers. There was a flurry of activity as students rushed to find a place to sit down.

The principal marched on to the stage and took up his customary position at the lectern. As the teachers sat down on chairs behind him, Mr Renton glared fiercely at the students as if daring one of them to talk.

He then took a newspaper from underneath his academic gown, and tapped the microphone on the lectern three times to make sure it was working: "Boom. Boom. Boom."

He usually started off his speeches with a complaint about student behaviour, and it appeared that today would be no different.

"I would like to bring to your attention the actions of someone sitting in this assembly …"

"Here we go," thought Fox. "I wonder who's in trouble now?"

"Where is Simon Phillips?" asked the principal in a stern voice.

Simon, who was sitting near Fox, went bright red and raised a trembling hand.

"Ooooh," said Mace, "looks like Porky's gonna get it!"

Mr Renton unfolded the *Davinal Digest* newspaper and held it up to reveal the front-page headline: "Local Boy Donates Time and Chocolates to Refugees".

"Simon has displayed an amazing amount of generosity," said Mr Renton, "by donating his time and also hundreds of dollars worth of chocolate bars to the refugee children at the old Davinal hospital."

Fox glanced over at Mace, whose eyes looked like they were about to pop out of their sockets.

WHAAAT?

"B-b-b-but ..." Mace stammered.

"How about a big round of applause for Simon Phillips?" said Mr Renton.

Everyone started clapping loudly. Everyone except for Mace.

"But they were *my* chocolate bars!" whined Mace. "I should be getting the credit for this."

"Don't worry," Vince said sympathetically. "I'll tell your dad that you were the one helping out the refugees."

"Shut up, Vince!" said Mace. That was the *last* thing his dad would want to hear.

Mace sat stewing in his seat as Mr Renton continued to say nice things about Simon.

"Is that steam coming out of Mace's ears?" asked Lewis with a smile. He cupped his hands as if they were a megaphone and said, "Stand back, I think he's about to blow!"

Lewis' comment made everyone in the row laugh. Even Vince snorted, which put Mace in an even fouler mood.

After the principal had finished praising Simon, he moved on to the next item on his agenda.

"At the start of the year, I put a note on the noticeboard calling for volunteers to put on a performance at assembly," he said. "I must say the response has been incredible."

In truth the response had been incredibly *bad*. Only two students had signed up and the first name on the list was "I.P. M'panz". When Mr Renton had gone into the teachers' staff room and called out, "Does anyone know I.P. M'panz?" all the teachers had cracked up with laughter.

"Come on, I need you to tell me if you know I.P. M'panz!" persisted Mr Renton, only making the teachers laugh even harder.

A passing student who had heard all the laughter and stopped to listen rushed outside to tell his friends. By lunchtime, word of Mr Renton's "I.P. M'panz" problem was spreading throughout the school.

Eventually Mr Renton realised what he was saying—

the name was a fake and had been put up on the board as a prank. In the end he'd had no choice but to choose the only other name on the list.

Mr Renton had hoped the volunteer performers would play the violin, perform as a barbershop quartet, or do some tap-dancing. But his first and only volunteer did none of these things.

Clearing his throat a little nervously, the principal said, "Our very first student to perform at assembly is Lewis Rioli—and he will be doing some stand-up comedy."

Lewis had not told any of friends about this, but Fox smiled warmly and slapped him on the back encouragingly as he walked by on his way to the stage.

Fox was amazed at how relaxed Lewis looked—in fact, he was grinning from ear to ear.

Lewis took the microphone from the holder on the lectern and walked casually to the middle of the stage.

"Wow, from up here you all look like ants!" he said, looking down at the audience.

Straight away everyone laughed.

"… without the antennae, obviously," he continued, "and hopefully you don't regurgitate your food into a liquid form like ants do—although you might after eating a pie from the tuck shop."

Lewis pretended to vomit and this set off the audience into howls of laughter. The food served at the school tuck shop was very unpopular—it was a brave student who took up the challenge of attempting to eat one of its rock-hard pies, in particular.

"They say only two things can survive a nuclear holocaust—cockroaches and the meat pies from the Davinal Primary tuck shop!"

Lewis went on to say, "So eventually only the pies would be left—because as soon as the cockroaches tried to eat one, they'd be goners, too!"

Lewis then did a hilarious impersonation of a cockroach eating a pie, then suddenly lay on his back

and spun around as if he was a dying beetle.

Lewis had to wait for the kids in the front row to stop laughing before he continued. Chung, who was sitting next to Fox, was chortling so hard he lost his balance and literally fell off his chair, which made him laugh even more.

"Hey, how can you tell if a fisherman is a goal umpire?" asked Lewis. "They always catch fish that are *this* long!" As Lewis said "this long" he put his fingers up like a goal umpire and everyone cracked up.

Vince snorted loudly and Mace shot him another withering look.

"We've got some great teachers here today," said Lewis, glancing over his shoulder at the teachers behind him, "and we've *also* got Mr Grinter!"

Mr Grinter was about to protest, but stopped when he spotted the principal slapping his knee and laughing.

"And speaking of Mr Grinter," said Lewis, "I'd like to finish off with a few impersonations."

Lewis then mimicked Mr Grinter's droning voice perfectly as he said, "Sorry I'm late ... um, my pet beagle died ... for the third time this week ... Why did it die? Because my voice is so boring ..."

Mr Renton roared with laughter as Lewis once again returned to his normal voice.

"And now let's hear from our principal."

Lewis drew a line down the middle of his hair to

represent Mr Renton's part. He then started talking with a clipped, stern voice that was exactly like the principal's.

"Tuck in your shirt—you've got a detention. Get off the grass—you've got a detention. Stop breathing air—you've got a detention."

Fox noticed that Mr Renton was still smiling, but it appeared to be somewhat forced. He clearly preferred it when Lewis was impersonating Mr Grinter.

"Can someone help me?" Lewis continued in Mr Renton's voice. "Does anybody know I.P. M'panz?"

By now the whole school had heard about what had happened in the staff room and all the students laughed at this. Even Mace let out a little chuckle before quickly pulling himself together and frowning.

The principal quickly stood up and started clapping.

"How about a big hand for Lewis Rioli?" he said, cutting Lewis off before he could embarrass him any further.

The students gave Lewis a standing ovation as he waved and walked off the stage. Even Vince started to stand up, but Mace grabbed him and dragged him back down.

"That was seriously awesome," said Fox as Lewis took his seat beside him.

Leaning over from her spot beside Chung, Paige whispered, "You put the fake name on the list and set this whole thing up, didn't you?"

Lewis grinned. "Who, me?" he said in his most innocent-sounding voice. "I have no idea what you're talking about."

"Settle down, everyone!" ordered Mr Renton. "I have an announcement to make about football."

The hall immediately fell dead silent.

"Cyril Rioli is coming back to our school to give a footy clinic tomorrow afternoon at 4pm—"

A huge cheer erupted from the students.

"Cyril was obviously so impressed with the way the school was run—" continued Mr Renton, puffing his chest out with pride.

But no one was listening.

"Assembly dismissed!" Mr Renton said huffily, and stormed off the stage. The other teachers, caught off guard by the principal's abrupt departure, all leapt up and scrambled after him.

"Excellent," said Fox, high-fiving Lewis. "How excited will Hugo be?"

"Pretty excited," said Lewis. "I think he just fainted!"

Mace was changing into his footy gear in the school's locker room when Chung walked over and put his bag down next to him.

"What do you think you're doing?" said Mace.

"Getting changed for the footy clinic," said Chung.

"I want to meet Cyril Rioli."

"As if Cyril Rioli will want to meet you!" said Mace, pulling his shirt over his head. "Anyway, don't put your bag there. You should get changed with your own kind."

"My own kind?" said Chung. "Oh, you mean humans."

This infuriated Mace, but he was still worried that Chung might pull the P.O.D. Grip on him so he simply snarled, "You'd better not get in my way out there, China Boy, because I'm going to run right through you!"

Mace had not been concentrating while changing into his footy gear, because Chung had distracted him.

"Hey Mace," said Chung, "your jumper is on inside out."

Mace looked down and saw Chung was right. He quickly ripped it off, turned it out the correct way and put it back on. Mace was thankful that Chung had told him—but not thankful enough to actually thank him!

Mace was determined to impress Cyril this time—especially after the humiliation he had suffered at last year's clinic, when his pants had slipped down to reveal his Thomas the Tank Engine underpants to the whole school. He headed outside and started to do some stretching exercises on the boundary line.

"There he is!" yelled out a third-grader as Cyril Rioli

jumped out of his car and starting walking towards the Davinal Primary oval.

The Diggers players all rushed over to Cyril and high-fived him.

When Cyril saw Lewis, he went over and gave his young cousin a hug.

"Good to catch up, cuz!" he said.

The Hawk star walked into the middle of the oval and called everyone in. Mace sprinted from the wing to make sure he was at the very front of the huddle. He was hoping Cyril had forgotten about the Thomas the Tank Engine wardrobe malfunction.

Mace managed to push a grade-two boy out of the way so he was as close as possible to the Hawthorn champion.

Cyril looked at him and said, "Hey, I know you— your name's *Thomas*, right?"

"Actually it's Mace."

"Sorry," said Cyril. "I don't know why I thought it was Thomas. Oh, that's right ..."

Then Cyril spotted Hugo in his bodysuit and called out, "How's my main man? Kicked any grubber goals lately?"

Fox quickly rushed around behind Hugo in case he was about to faint again, but Hugo managed to stay upright. "Yes, no—I mean, I don't know," he stammered.

"And he's the super-smart one!" said Lewis, winking at Cyril.

The clinic was a great success, and Mace was feeling particularly smug afterwards thanks to his accurate kicking and handballing throughout the session. "Maybe Cyril will tell the AFL talent scouts about me," he thought.

To finish up, Cyril decided that the older kids would do some one-on-one marking drills. The kids formed into pairs and got into a line. Cyril then kicked the ball high in the air, and one by one each pair competed for the mark.

"Try to put yourself in a good position," instructed Cyril. "But if you can't mark the ball, try to prevent your opponent from marking by punching the ball to the ground."

Mace looked around and could not believe his luck. Standing next to him was Chung.

"Ha—Chung!" thought Mace. "He's half my height and weighs about 10 kilograms—this will be *so* easy!"

Just before Cyril kicked the ball, Chung said, "Ooh, my shoelace is undone—can someone please take my place?"

"I will!" said Fox.

The cocky expression quickly vanished from Mace's face.

Even before the ball went up in the air, Mace knew exactly what was about to happen. He felt Fox's knee on his shoulder as he launched himself skyward, and heard the rest of the kids clapping and cheering even before the Diggers captain had hit the ground.

"Brilliant mark, Fox!" said Cyril. "Great skills!"

Mace trudged to the back of the queue—making sure he was next to Chung this time.

But once again, as they reached the front of the line, Chung announced that his shoelace was undone and asked someone to go in his place. This time Simon volunteered.

As the ball came down towards them, Simon took the front position. Mace was desperate to impress Cyril, but the Diggers full-forward was too tall and strong to get around, so he decided to try taking a specky from behind Simon. But Mace's timing was slightly off and he jumped too early, and Simon marked the ball cleanly in his outstretched hands.

"Mace, if you're not in a position to mark, try to punch the ball away, okay?" advised Cyril.

The next time Mace and Chung got to the front of the queue, Chung declared that he had swallowed a fly, so Bruno stepped up in his place.

Mace rolled his eyes in disbelief. "You can't be serious!" he yelled at Chung.

"Here it comes," called out Cyril as he kicked the ball high into the air.

On this occasion, Mace used his body perfectly to take the front position. He was all set to take the mark when Bruno punched the ball away at the last moment.

"Well done, Bruno!" said Cyril. "That is a perfect example of what I was talking about."

Mace was fuming as he returned to the back of the queue, determined not to let Chung trick him again.

When they reached the front of the line, before he had a chance to make any more excuses, Mace grabbed Chung's arm and snarled, "Not this time you don't."

Cyril kicked the ball high in the air and Mace got into position. Mace knew he had this one in the bag. But just as he was about to leap up and take a simple **overhead mark**, Chung called out, "Hey Mace, your pants have fallen down!" In a panic, Mace looked down—and while he was distracted Chung took the easiest of **chest marks**.

Mace's pants had not really fallen down, so it looked like he was simply being lazy.

"You have to at least try, Mace," said Cyril.

"I wasn't ready!" said Mace. "We have to do that one again!"

"This time I'm going to thrash you, you puny little twerp!" he whispered to Chung.

Cyril kicked the ball into the air and, using his superior body strength, Mace held out Chung and took a well-judged overhead mark. "Check this out, everyone— Mace is in da house!" he cried arrogantly, waving the ball above his head like a trophy.

Unfortunately for Mace, this time his pants really *had* fallen down.

Looking south, Mace was horrified to discover that he was wearing underpants with Bob the Builder pictures on them.

"These aren't mine!" he cried in alarm. "I swear I've never seen these underpants before in my life!"

"Are you quite sure about that, Mace?" asked Chung. But he posed the question with such a cheeky grin that Fox began to suspect his new friend was behind this—even though he couldn't imagine how he'd done it.

Just when Mace thought the situation couldn't get any more humiliating, a first-grader walked over to him and said, "Don't worry, mate—I still like Bob the Builder, too."

7

A Rosie Future

After hearing Lewis' impersonation at assembly the day before, Mr Grinter decided he needed to be more entertaining in the classroom. So the next day at school, he started off the history lesson by telling a joke.

In his usual droning voice, he said, "What do you call a magpie that is an Impressionist artist?"

Vince put up his hand and asked, "Is this going to be on a test?"

"No, no," said Mr Grinter impatiently, "it's a joke."

The students had never heard their incredibly boring teacher even try to tell a joke before, so they were a little confused.

"You give up?" asked Mr Grinter. "Okay, its name would be ... wait for it ... Pablo *Peck*-casso!"

When Mr Grinter had practised this joke in front of the mirror, he had assumed the punchline would be met with lots of loud laughter. But now, as the students stared back at him blankly, all he could hear were the cicadas singing outside.

"*Peck*-casso. Get it? Because you know, Pablo *Picasso* was a painter and magpies, you know, they peck people," he said, making a pecking motion with his hand to help explain the joke.

Two hands shot up into the air.

"You can take this one, Hugo," said Chung, putting his hand back down.

"Mr Grinter, the artist Pablo Picasso was born after the Impressionist era had finished," said Hugo. "So the joke doesn't really make sense."

Sally was just starting to write down a comment about Mr Grinter in her notebook when there was a knock at the door.

SCALE

0   ·5   1

metres

"Come in!" called out Mr Grinter, welcoming the distraction.

The door opened and into the class walked a tall, athletic girl with golden-brown hair that was tied back into a long, plaited ponytail.

"Ah, you must be the new girl," said Mr Grinter,

looking down at a list on his desk. "Yes, here it is—Rosie McHusky. Class, this is Rosie McHusky."

Rosie smiled, gave a quick wave and said, "Hey."

"Nice ponytail!" called out Mace with a snigger.

Still smiling, Rosie's flicked her ponytail from side to side, looked Mace right in the eyes and said, "Can you fix it … Bob?"

The whole class roared with laughter and Mace went bright red.

"How could she know about the undies incident?" he thought. "She's only been at the school for 20 seconds."

As it turned out, Rosie's dad was in the army. And last night her family had eaten at the Riolis' place, because Lewis' father was also in the army. Over dinner, Lewis had got Rosie up to date with all the latest school gossip, including Mace's special Bob the Builder underwear.

"She got you a beauty there, Mace," said Vince.

"No she didn't," said Mace defensively. "My ponytail line was much funnier."

"Then how come no one laughed?"

"Shut up, Vince," said Mace.

Fox watched Rosie as she sat down at the empty desk next to Paige.

"Mmm, Rosie McHusky … I know that name from somewhere," he thought.

Fox didn't spend too much time thinking about where

he might have seen Rosie before, though—he had far more important matters to daydream about. Tonight was the Diggers' first training session!

He wasn't the only one who was buzzing with excitement. At morning tea Fox overheard Paige telling the new girl how much fun it was to play with the Diggers.

"Get this," she was saying. "Our mascot is a kangaroo—an actual kangaroo!"

"Cool!" said Rosie.

Tonight was also the first training session for the Dragons, and Mace couldn't wait to see all the superstar talent that his father had assembled.

"Imagine how good training will be with no losers to muck up the drills," he said to Vince.

"Yeah!" said Vince. "Oh, by the way, even with all these star players, I'll still be vice-captain, right?"

"Um, err, well … Hey, did you want my dad to give you a lift to training tonight?" said Mace, quickly changing the subject.

Fortunately Vince had a very short attention span.

"A lift in your dad's sports car? Excellent!"

Mr Winter picked up Mace and Vince straight after school and said, "I need to pop into the bank on the way—it won't take long."

Miles had to visit the bank because the parents of all

the star Dragons recruits were demanding more money. They told him that the cash they had received was only for their boys *signing up* for the Dragons, and that if Miles wanted their boys to train as well then he would have to pay them a "training fee".

The town of Davinal only had one bank. It was very small and run by a timid man called Mr Shloogal.

As soon as Mr Shloogal saw Miles Winter arrive with two boys trailing behind him, he began to perspire nervously. He was scared of Miles.

"How can I help you today, Mr Winter?" asked Mr Shloogal in a trembling voice.

"By not asking me stupid questions," snapped Miles.

Vince watched closely as Miles proceeded to fill out a withdrawal slip. "Hey Mr Winter, how come you're taking money out of the 'Tilley Fawcett Inheritance Trust Account'?"

Miles' face turned red and he looked around nervously to make sure no one had heard Vince.

"Shh!" he whispered. "It's all above board."

It wasn't.

About a year ago, one of Miles' clients by the name of Beverly Stephenson had died. In her will, she had left Miles strict instructions:

Dear Mr Winter,

I have no living relatives so I wish for all my money to be given to Ms Tilley Fawcett. Tilley very kindly looked after me when I was sick many years ago. I have lost touch with her, but have never forgotten her kindness. You are to track down Tilley Fawcett and give her all of my money and all of my thanks,

Yours sincerely,

Ms Beverly Stephenson

Miles had never heard of a Tilley Fawcett—and frankly did not try very hard to track her down. All he did was put a very cheap ad in the *Davinal Digest* that read:

"If u r Tilley Fawcett, ring this number: ..."

The fact that he placed the tiny ad on page 43 in a section called "Discount Fortune-telling Services" made it highly unlikely that anyone would ever see it.

In the end no one claiming to be Tilley Fawcett had contacted Miles, so he'd put all of Beverly's money in a special bank account called the "Tilley Fawcett Inheritance Trust Account".

"Tilley Fawcett will probably never come forward and ask for her money," thought Miles. "And if she was as old as Beverly Stephenson, there's a good chance she's no longer with us anyway."

Miles' legal business had been struggling ever since the Swifts had moved to town, as many of his clients preferred to deal with them. So Miles thought it would be okay if he occasionally "borrowed" some money from the Tilley Fawcett Inheritance Trust Account.

He would definitely pay it all back—as soon as his business picked up again.

Miles walked over to the teller's window, handed Mr Shloogal the withdrawal slip and said, "I need this amount of cash and also a printout of how much money is left in the account."

Mr Shloogal looked at the withdrawal slip and mopped the perspiration from his brow. He wasn't really sure that Miles should be taking cash out of this account.

"Hurry up, or we'll be late for training," barked Miles.

Mr Shloogal quickly keyed the withdrawal details into his computer, then handed Mr Winter a pile of notes and a receipt revealing the account balance.

As they walked out of the bank, Miles accidentally dropped the receipt, and Vince helpfully stooped down to pick it up.

After inspecting the piece of paper, Vince's eyes widened.

"Oh my God, there's over a million dollars in this account!" he said at the top of his voice. "Who is this Tilley Fawcett?"

"Shhhhhhh!" said Miles.

Then, in his most charming voice, he said, "You know, Vince, I've been thinking—you should definitely be the vice-captain of the Dragons this year."

"You ripper!" said Vince, immediately forgetting all about the Tilley Fawcett Inheritance Trust Account.

After school, Rosie McHusky went home and changed into her running gear. She had really enjoyed talking to Paige about the Diggers at morning recess, and decided to jog down and check out training. Rosie had never played a game of football before, but she had played kick-to-kick in the backyard with her older brothers since she was three. Well, until about a year ago, when her brothers refused to keep playing with her because she was so much better than them!

Rosie had noticed a football oval when her family first drove into Davinal, and had assumed it was the Diggers' home ground. But when she ran on to the oval, she was surprised to come face to face with Mace Winter and his Dragons teammates.

"Oops, I'm guessing this isn't the Diggers' home ground," she thought.

Mace was still fuming over Rosie's "Bob the Builder" line in class that morning.

"Don't even think about training with the Dragons— we have a 'no chicks' policy!" he said.

"Yeah, why don't ya play for the Diggers, loser— they're 5 kilometres that way!" said Vince, pointing his finger to the west.

Rosie smiled.

"That's fine," she said sweetly. "You won't mind if

I borrow a ball, will you?"

Rosie casually picked up a footy that was lying on the oval and slowly jogged off.

"She's stealing a Dragons football!" screamed Mace. "Let's get her!"

With 25 boys in hot pursuit, Rosie increased her speed and was soon going so fast her ponytail was flying straight out behind her.

"She's only a girl," yelled Mace. "We'll catch her for sure."

But, if anything, as Rosie raced in and out of the trees that were dotted around the oval, the distance between her and her pursuers was increasing.

"She's running way too fast—she'll conk out soon," puffed Mace.

Mace's hopes were dashed when Rosie lifted her pace yet again, and the 25 Dragons players who had been chasing her began to drop off one by one. Finally Mace gave up, too, and fell on the ground panting.

He watched as Rosie ran back on to the oval, slotted a perfect drop-punt goal from the boundary, and then sped off into the night.

Vince sucked in some deep breaths and staggered over to Mace.

"Maybe we should review that 'no chicks' policy?"

"Shut up, Vince!"

Over the other side of town, Fox was excited to be back at training with the Diggers. He waved to Lewis, who was leaning against the boundary fence with his sketchpad, then went around greeting the rest of the players.

"Hey, how's it going?" he asked Mo Officer, who had grown over the break and was looking even stronger than last year.

"Nabaceptfacatulprizecac'plaintho," mumbled Mo.

Fox had absolutely no idea what had just been said to him, but fortunately Paige was nearby—she always understood Mo, and was able to translate.

"He said things have been going quite well, apart from a fall in the price of cattle—not that he's complaining, though."

"Yep, that's what I thought he said," said Fox, with a laugh.

Chung arrived at training and Fox took him over to meet the Diggers' coach.

"Mr Scott, this is Chung—he's pretty much untackleable," said Fox, not sure whether "untackleable" was actually a word. ("It's not," Hugo assured him later.)

"Welcome to the Diggers," said Mr Scott as he shook Chung's hand. "Thanks for joining the team!"

Chung was made to feel very welcome, especially when Joey hopped over and gave him a high paw.

Fox looked over to the other side of the oval and saw a girl with a ponytail and a perfect running style moving towards him at great speed—it was Rosie McHusky.

Fox suddenly realised where he'd heard her name before. Late last year he had gone along to watch Lewis compete at a national athletics tournament. Lewis had broken the Australian record for his age group in both the 100- and 200-metre sprints, and Fox had been thrilled for his best mate.

But someone else had also smashed a number of Australian records that day—in the 800-, 1500- and 3000-metre events. As Fox and Lewis were leaving the athletics stadium, her name had been announced over the loudspeaker: Rosie McHusky.

As she continued to speed towards him, Rosie swooped on a football, barely breaking stride, and **drilled** a low, left-foot drop-punt pass straight on to Fox's chest.

Fox was gobsmacked. All he could think to say when Rosie ran up to him was, "Um, are you a **left-footer?**"

"No, a right-footer," said Rosie, with a smile.

"Oh my God," thought Fox before turning to his coach and saying, "Mr Scott, I'd like to introduce you to the Diggers' new ruck-rover, Rosie McHusky."

Mr Scott shook Rosie's hand and then, looking over towards Joey, said with a laugh, "And it looks like we've picked up *another* new recruit."

Fox laughed as well when he saw that Gary the

rabbit and Joey were sniffing each other cautiously. When these formalities were out of the way, the two of them started acting like old friends.

GARY
Hitches
a
RIDE

The Diggers captain glanced over to the changing rooms and was pleased to see the arrival of five new players who had played for the Dragons last year.

"Looks like we won't have a problem fielding a full team this year," thought Fox.

Mr Scott called everyone in and officially welcomed Rosie, Chung and the other new players to the Diggers.

"Make sure you introduce yourselves to these new guys if you don't already know them," he said. "And even if you do know them, still say hi."

Everyone immediately yelled out "Hi!" and Mr Scott smiled.

"Cyril Rioli has kindly sent us through a new drill," said the coach. "I want you to all spread out around the boundary line and we are going to do some circle work.

"What you will do is start off moving clockwise, then I want one person to take the ball and kick it to someone leading ahead of them. When that person takes the mark they must handball—not kick, but handball— to a player running past. That player will then kick it to a teammate, who will mark the ball and handball it to a player running by. So it's kick, handball, kick, handball—you got that?"

"Yes!" yelled the Diggers players enthusiastically as they spread out around the oval.

Fox was rapt to see Chris and Sammy combining beautifully with Rosie, and Paige kicking perfectly to Simon Phillips. He noted that Mo still always passed the ball with a torpedo punt, and that he was as accurate as ever.

Chung's enthusiasm was infectious. He called loudly for the ball and showed an enormous burst of speed every time he received a handball or a kick. The only problem was that once he had the ball, he didn't know how to pass it on to his teammates. Mr Scott picked this up straight away and called him in to demonstrate how to handball and kick. He then practised short passes with Chung one-on-one as the rest of the team continued with the circle work.

After 15 minutes the players were exhausted, so the coach called them in to the middle of the ground. As they got their breath back, Mr Scott gave them some general tips.

"Always back up your teammate. If you run past and don't receive the handball, keep running and you may get it next time. Keep your eyes on the ball as you drop it on to your boot, not on where you're trying to kick it."

Mr Scott then sent the players back out, saying, "This time, let's move the ball anti-clockwise."

After the Diggers got the hang of running in a different direction, the coach instructed them to change the angles of their kicking and running patterns.

"Sometimes kick the ball sideways—it makes you unpredictable and you'll confuse the opposition!" he called out, remembering Cyril's advice.

Fox could not stop smiling. He loved being back at training and couldn't wait for the Diggers' first game.

Near the end of the session, Mr Scott brought all the players into a huddle. Just as he was about to say a few words, Mr Percy appeared next to him, holding a clipboard.

"Sorry I'm a little late—no biggie," he said. "Okay, everyone get down and give me five chin-ups!"

Mr Scott didn't know what to say, and neither did the players, who were completely confused by Mr Percy's ridiculous request.

"Okay, you can just do two chin-ups," said Mr Percy.

The ex-Diggers coach suddenly heard a series of dull thuds approaching him from behind.

"Uh-oh!" he said, before sprinting off the oval with both Joey and Gary the rabbit hot on his heels.

The Diggers players all cracked up with laughter.

"Yes, it's definitely good to be back," thought Fox.

8

Let the Games Begin

On the morning of the Diggers' first game of the season, Fox woke early. Very early. He looked at the radio alarm clock by his bed.

"Huh, 1am? No way!"

He managed to get back to sleep, but then woke up in a panic after dreaming he had slept in and missed the game. He glanced over to check the time on the clock again—it was 1.12am.

"At this rate I'll never get any sleep," he thought. "I'll be so tired I won't be able to—"

The next thing Fox knew, it was 7am and his alarm was waking him up.

He bounced out of bed and went over to his desk, where he had neatly laid out his footy gear the night before. He loved the Diggers jumper, which had a blue background with a yellow sash and yellow trim on the V neck.

Fox entered the kitchen to find Chase already halfway through a bowl of cereal. His younger brother put down his spoon and immediately fired off a string of questions without stopping for breath.

"Do you think you can beat the Tennant Hill Tigers? How many goals will Simon kick? How will Chung and Rosie go in their first games? Where will Paige line up? Who do you reckon will take the biggest specky? And what flavour cordial will you get at quarter-time?"

Fox paused before replying in an equally quickfire manner: "Yes, seven, really well, half-forward flank, Sammy or Chris, raspberry or lime—but I'm hoping for raspberry."

Mr Swift, who had walked in just in time to hear this rather unusual answer, was standing behind Fox with a puzzled look on his face.

"Have you guys invented a new language?" he asked.

"No, Dad—we were just talking about today's game," said Fox.

"Oh yes, best of luck," said Mr Swift. "I, um, really hope you win the, er, **contested ball,** kick the footy down the, umm, **corridor,** and put some, er, scoreboard pressure on your opponents."

Fox and Chase looked at each other in amazement. Their dad knew absolutely nothing about football, and it was a shock to hear him actually making sense for a change.

"Dad, have you been googling 'footy terms'?" Fox asked suspiciously.

"What are you talking about?" said Mr Swift defensively.

Chase snatched his dad's mobile phone from his hand and quickly checked the search history

"Mmm, what do we have here?" he asked with a smile. "'Footy terms you can use to impress people'—what do you say about that, Dad?"

"I refuse to say anything without my lawyer being present!" he replied.

"I'm not disappointed that you used Google," said Fox, imitating his father. "I'm just disappointed you had to fib about it."

"What's going on?" asked Mrs Swift as she entered the kitchen.

"I was just telling the boys what a wonderful mother you are," said Mr Swift, with a wink.

"That's not true!" said Chase.

"What's that, Chase?" asked Mr Swift. "You don't think your mum is a wonderful mother?"

Mrs Swift looked at Chase as if she were upset, and put her hands on her hips.

"No Mum, I mean yes, I mean, I didn't mean ..." mumbled Chase, looking over at his brother for help.

"You're on your own, bro," said Fox, with a smile.

Fox was so excited about playing football again he arrived at the Diggers changing rooms half an hour early. Mr Scott was already there writing the players' positions up on the giant whiteboard on the wall.

"Hey Fox," said Mr Scott, "all set for a big start to the season?"

"You bet," said Fox, picking up a *Football Record* from the pile sitting on the table and turning to the 'On This Day' page like he'd done every game last season.

As usual, there was a paragraph that referred to Mr Scott when he was playing for the Davinal Diggers **seniors**:

> On this day 40 years ago … the Diggers' young champion Greg Scott played another blinder of a game in his club's comfortable win over the Stingrays. Despite playing in defence, Scott managed to kick seven goals, including two towering torpedo punts from near the centre of the ground. His creativity and speed brought his teammates into the game, and the Diggers recorded a strong 63-point victory. Scott is set to have a highly successful career as a professional footballer—he is simply that good.

Fox felt really sad for his coach. "Mr Scott was so

unlucky to hurt his knee," he thought.

As if he could read Fox's mind, Mr Scott said, "Hey, don't feel sorry for me. I should have had a back-up plan."

"What do you mean?" asked Fox.

"You can't just assume you'll end up playing in the big League and put all your eggs in that basket," explained the coach. "You need to think about other jobs you could do, just in case things don't work out."

Fox nodded and tried to think about what he would like to do apart from play football.

"Maybe I could be a lion tamer?" he said.

"Mmm, probably good to have a back-up plan for your back-up plan," said Mr Scott, which made them both laugh.

The other Diggers players began to file into the changing rooms. Everyone was excited about the first game of the season and chatted noisily as they changed into their footy gear.

Lewis walked over to Fox and patted him on the back.

"Fooks Swift," he said in a broad Scottish accent, "yer haff ta show sum bravery tuday, lad!"

"Aye laddie," he continued, raising his voice, "ya haff ter git the hard ball, Fooks, ya haff ta get the hard ball! And if ya don't, I'll be telling the Loch Ness Monsta on yer—or my name's noot Larry McLarry of the clan called McLarry!"

Everyone loved it, and Fox high-fived Lewis.

"And by tha way, ma brother's name is Barry!" added Lewis, causing another round of laughter.

"Hey Lewis, how come you're not in your footy jumper?" asked Fox.

"Now that the Diggers have so many players, you don't need me any more," said Lewis in his normal voice. "And so Mr Scott has made me the team's **runner**."

"Excellent!" said Fox, thinking how much fun it would be to receive the coach's messages in a Scottish accent.

Mr Scott called for some quiet and asked the players to gather around him.

"Okay, it's the first game of the season—are you guys pumped?" he asked.

"Yes!" yelled out the Diggers players.

"That's good, because I'm sure the Tigers will be pretty pumped too. It's brilliant we have so many new recruits this year—how about we give all the 'newbies' a huge clap?"

The original Diggers players clapped enthusiastically, and there were several thunderous "whoo-hoos".

"Because we have new players this year, there will be a lot more players on the bench. Just to be clear, everyone will play at least three full quarters each game. But to make sure this happens, I'll need to take quite a few players off at the end of each quarter. And it doesn't matter how good you are or how well you're playing, you will all be spending time on the bench this year, okay?"

"What, even Fox?" asked Simon.

"Yes, even Fox," replied Mr Scott.

Fox had never sat on the bench in his life, and while this was disappointing news, he knew it was only fair— and as captain of the team he had to be positive and support his coach. All his teammates were looking at him, waiting for his reaction.

"That's totally cool," he said.

"Great," said Mr Scott. "Now I want you all to go out there and play as a team—lots of talk and helping each other out."

"Come on, guys!" said Fox, rising to his feet.

"Yeah, come on, Diggers!" yelled out his teammates.

And with that, Joey and Gary the rabbit led the players out on to the oval, where they were met with the cheers of the loyal Diggers supporters.

As the Diggers warmed up and did their pre-match stretching exercises, Gary ran around them at blistering speed, and when Fox went over to shake hands and flip the coin with the Tennant Hill Tigers captain, Joey went with him to give her support.

"I really hope I win more tosses this year," thought Fox as the umpire flicked the 50-cent piece into the air.

"Heads!" yelled out the captain of the Tigers.

"Come on tails," thought Fox.

"Heads it is," said the umpire.

"Darn!" thought Fox.

"We'll kick that way," said the Tennant Hill skipper, pointing to the northern end of the ground. Fox was happy about that because he'd been hoping to kick to the southern end first anyway.

"It's sort of like I won the toss," he told himself.

The Diggers took up their positions, with Sammy, Rosie, Chung and Fox starting in the middle.

The umpire bounced the ball and Sammy, who was a lot taller than the opposing ruck, palmed it easily to Fox, who handballed to Rosie. The Diggers' new ruck-rover sped off and kicked a long pass to Simon, who had led out from full-forward. Simon then **dished off** a handball to the helmet-wearing Paige, who flashed by and snapped a beautiful right-foot goal. The crowd roared and those in cars honked their horns as Paige did a series of celebratory cartwheels.

The Wheelie Amazing
PAIGE TURNER

"That has to be the best start to a season ever in the history of football," thought Fox.

Thanks to the domination of Sammy and Chris in the ruck, the Diggers ended up with the footy whenever there was a ball-up. Rosie was incredibly impressive, too—she ran like lightning without seeming to tire, and passed the ball beautifully into their forward line. It was also great to see Chung with the footy in his hands—he was impossible to tackle, as Fox had suspected he would be, and even though he made a few mistakes with his kicking and handballing it was clear he was going to be a cracking footballer sooner rather than later.

At quarter-time Fox checked the scoreboard and the Diggers led the Tigers easily.

Diggers: 6.2 (38)
Visitors: 1.3 (9)

In the quarter-time **huddle** Mr Scott praised the Diggers for all their hard work, especially the new players.

"Great effort, everyone … Chung and Rosie are creating fantastic drive in the middle … Keep talking to each other and if someone does something good, make sure you congratulate them."

Before the players ran back out to their positions, he announced who would be coming off the ground in the second quarter.

"Bruno, Rosie, Paige, Chris, Mo … and Fox."

With these six star players on the bench, the game completely changed in the second quarter. The Tennant Hill players gained confidence as the Diggers started making mistakes.

Simon Phillips was still on the ground, but the ball rarely made it to him at full-forward. The Tigers managed to kick five goals in a row, and took the lead just before half-time.

The father of one of the players who had come across from the Dragons was irate. His name was Mr Lemon, and he started yelling and screaming at Mr Scott.

"Are you blind?!" he yelled. "Put the good players

back on—we're getting killed."

Mr Scott ignored him, but Mr Lemon just continued with the abuse.

"You're useless, coach! Take off the no-hopers and put on the stars!"

When the half-time siren sounded, the Diggers were trailing by five points.

Diggers: 6.4 (40)
Visitors: 6.9 (45)

Mr Scott told his players to head to the changing rooms and grab a drink of cordial. But instead of joining them, he strode over to where the angry Mr Lemon was standing with his arms crossed.

"Listen, mate—lose the attitude," said Mr Scott.

"How dare you?!" started Mr Lemon, but Mr Scott cut him off.

"I am trying to give every kid on the Diggers list a chance to improve his or her skills and develop as a footballer—and that includes your son Leo."

"But, but—"

"No 'buts'—this is junior football, not AFL seniors. These kids should be having fun, which is difficult for Leo to do when his dad is screaming out in front of everyone and behaving like a complete jerk." And with that, Mr Scott headed to the changing rooms to talk to his team, leaving Mr Lemon to fume on the boundary line.

Mr Lemon's wife, who had just arrived at the ground, went over to see what the coach had been talking to her husband about.

"What's going on?" she asked.

"I was just yelling out a few home truths," replied Mr Lemon, "and then that Greg Scott bloke came over and was completely unreasonable."

Mrs Lemon rolled her eyes. She had heard her husband's "home truths" before.

"So what did Mr Scott say?" she asked.

"He had the nerve to say I was embarrassing Leo by yelling out stuff," said Mr Lemon. "And wait until you get a load of *this*—he said footy at this level is all about the kids having fun and improving their skills."

Mrs Lemon folded her arms, raised her eyebrows and stared at her husband. Mr Lemon had seen that look in his wife's eyes before and knew he was in a lot of trouble.

"You know, now that I think about it, Mr Scott may have had a point," reflected Mr Lemon.

"And what are you going to say to Mr Scott when he comes out after half-time?"

"Um … 'Sorry for being a complete jerk'?"

"That's right, honey—off you go."

Mr Scott put the six star players back on the field in the third quarter, and the Diggers once again took control of the game. Fox took an amazing mark in the goalsquare, sitting on his opponent's shoulder, and then somehow managed to kick the ball through the goals before he hit the ground.

Lewis ran out to pass on a message from the coach, which he delivered it in a French accent.

"*Sacrebleu, Monsieur Le Fox!* Zat goal was *magnifique*—you flew higher zan ze Eiffel Tower—ooh la la, *crêpes Suzette!*"

"Crêpes Suzette?" said Fox with a puzzled look on his face.

"I am so sorry, Monsieur, 'crêpes Suzette' was ze only uzzer French word I could zink of … *Au revoir!*"

Just before three-quarter time, Hugo went for a mark but misjudged the flight of the ball, which hit him fair and square on his head. This is called a "**falcon**"—and is not only painful, but also extremely embarrassing.

To make matters worse for Hugo, he hadn't managed a kick or a handball for the entire match, and it was his turn to sit on the bench in the last quarter.

"Don't worry about it, Hugo—you'll mark it next time," said Fox, rushing over to his friend.

When the siren sounded, the scoreboard showed the Diggers had a handy lead.

Diggers: 11.8 (74)
Visitors: 7.11 (53)

Mr Scott encouraged the team to look for Simon's leads when kicking into the forward line, and Paige to be ready to grab the crumbs if the ball hit the **deck**. He praised Bruno, Mo and the other defenders for restricting the Tigers to just one goal, and Sammy, Chris, Fox, Rosie and Chung for their fine work in the middle of the ground.

Mr Scott knew that Hugo was feeling down about his game, and called him over just before the teams went back out to start the final quarter.

"Hey Hugo," he said, "I wouldn't mind your advice on a couple of moves in this last quarter, if that's okay?"

Hugo's face lit up. "Really?" he said.

"Definitely. I think you've got a really good football brain when it comes to strategy—in fact, would you be interested in being my assistant coach?"

"That would be so cool!" said Hugo.

Fox watched Mr Scott helping out Hugo, and once again marvelled at what a sensational coach he had.

The home team went on to win the game by 39 points, and Fox looked at the scoreboard with great satisfaction.

Diggers: 16.11 (107)

Visitors: 9.14 (68)

Fox was rapt that the Diggers had started off their season with such a solid win. They had picked up a champion ruck-rover in Rosie, and Fox was confident that Chung would be a star player by the end of the season.

Not only that, but Chris and Sammy were even better than last year, and Mo, Bruno, Paige and Simon had all taken their games to a new level.

"I really think we can beat the Dragons," thought Fox as he walked around the field shaking hands with the Tennant Hill Tigers players. "I guess we'll find out next week when we play them."

But after reading the local newspaper the next day, Fox wasn't quite so confident.

Davinal Dragons 32.25 (217) d Firbush Fever 2.2 (14).

"Wow!" thought Fox, "The Dragons won by more than 200 points."

He looked more closely at the results and saw that a player named Jackson had kicked nine goals and been named in the best players.

"That's odd," thought Fox. "The Dragons didn't have a player named Jackson last year—there was that Jacko guy who played for the Colbran Cockatoos, though. Hmm …"

Fox noticed some other new surnames in the Dragons' best players: Rodan, Westin, Lucas …

Then the penny dropped.

There had been a star on-baller called Peter Rodan playing for the Romana Roosters last year; Seb Westin had been a champion full-back for the Stingrays; and

Tony Lucas had been a really clever goal sneak for the Tennant Hill Tigers. Somehow the Dragons had managed to steal all the best players from the other teams in the competition.

"No wonder they won by 200 points," Fox said out loud.

Before class started on Monday morning, Mace and Vince were behaving as arrogantly as—well, Mace and Vince.

"Woohoo, 203 points!" said Mace. "And we didn't even try in the last quarter."

"No wonder everyone's calling us 'The Unbeatables'," said Vince.

"Everyone?" said Lewis. "I'm pretty sure it's just you two."

"Not true!" said Vince. "Mace's dad does as well, so that's *three* of us!"

"And after we wipe the floor with the Diggers next week, you'll be saying it too," crowed Mace.

"Isn't it interesting that so many star players from other clubs are happy to travel so far to play with the Dragons this year," said Fox.

"It's not really surprising," said Mace. "Everyone wants to play for the Dragons because we're the best."

"Yeah," said Vince. "It's because we're totally awesome."

"Ha!" said Fox. "Mace, we all know the only reason those guys are playing for the Dragons is because your dad is paying them."

"Even if that's true, you can't prove it," said Mace smugly.

"Yeah, you can't prove it!" echoed Vince.

"Hey Vince, how does it feel to be the only Dragons player not being paid?" asked Lewis.

"That's not true!" said Vince defiantly. "Mace isn't being paid either!"

"Shut up, Vince!"

Mace stormed back to his desk with Vince hot on his heels.

"You're not being paid, are you, Mace? You'd tell me if you were ... wouldn't you?" said Vince as Fox and Lewis burst out laughing.

9

Snappy

When Fox turned up at the Dragons ground on the next Saturday morning, Mace and Vince were waiting for him.

"You are so going to get thrashed today," said Mace.

"Yeah ... because ... the Diggers are so, umm ... err ... stupid!" said Vince, who wasn't very good at making up witty lines on the spot.

"If you want to see something *really* stupid, go take a look in the mirror," said Fox.

"But if I look in the mirror I'll just see my own reflection," said Vince. "Ohhhh ..."

"Shut up, Vince!" said Mace.

Mace was about to make a few more nasty comments, but the arrival of Sammy and Chris made him think better of it. He hightailed it into the changing rooms, with Vince close behind him.

As Fox high-fived his mates hello, he said with a smile,

"Who are you two going to play like today?"

"Nic Nat!" said Sammy and Chris together.

Fox entered the visitors' changing rooms, said hi to Mr Scott, and picked up a copy of the *Record*.

On the 'On This Day' page there was a series of three grainy black-and-white photos. On closer inspection, Fox realised they were action shots of Mr Scott taking the most amazing mark Fox had ever seen.

> On this day 40 years ago ... Davinal Diggers high-flyer Greg Scott took what many believe to have been the mark of the century.
>
> In the second-round match against the Gregtown Goannas, Scott flew into the air to take a screamer on the shoulders of the Goannas full-back when a sudden wind shift changed the direction of the ball. The Diggers' champion stretched out and balanced the ball on the fingertips of his right hand and, as he was falling back to the ground, rolled the ball down the back of his hand and all the way along his arm. Then, with a flick of his shoulder, Scott popped the ball up and pulled it to his chest. From that day on, this **grab** would become known as "The Mark".

Fox looked up from the record and glanced at Mr Scott, who was patiently showing Chung how to kick a drop punt.

"How cool would it have been to play in the same team as Mr Scott?" he said to Lewis, who had just arrived.

"Yeah," said Lewis, "but think about how old you'd be!"

Young Fox   Silver Fox

Later on, after all the players had changed, Mr Scott called them over and delivered his pre-match speech.

"I know how badly you guys want to win this one—"

"Yeah!" yelled out a number of the Diggers.

"All I'm asking is for you to give your absolute best, okay?"

This time the whole team cried out, "Yeah!"

"Cum'ndigs," added Mo.

"And if you do that, win, lose or draw you can walk off the ground with your heads held high," said Mr Scott.

"Let's give it everything!" yelled Fox, standing up and bouncing around on the balls of his feet. He could not wait to get out on to the oval and start playing.

The rest of the team jumped up and started deliberately bumping into each other as they shouted out words of encouragement.

"Tackle hard, Diggers!"

"Play in front!"

"Back each other up!"

"Lots of talk out there!"

With the team all fired up and ready to go, Fox led them through the changing-room door. Joey joined him at the front of the pack and hopped out on to the oval, to the delight of the large group of spectators.

"Hmm, I wonder where Gary the rabbit is this week," said Fox.

"Maybe he's caught up in traffic?" said Lewis.

While his teammates did some stretching exercises, Fox went to the middle of the ground to toss the coin.

As captain of the Dragons, Mace also ran over for the toss, and tried to "accidentally" bump into Fox as he went past—but Fox stepped backwards at the last second, which caused Mace to stumble and fall.

"Hey Mace, did you have a nice *trip*?!" yelled out Lewis.

The umpire held up a coin, flipped it into the air and said, "Diggers' call!"

"Tails," said Fox, crossing his fingers behind his back.

"And it's ... heads," said the umpire after examining the coin.

"Yesssssss! In your face, Swift, ya loser!" said Mace, jumping around like a maniac and pointing in the direction he wanted his team to kick to in the first quarter.

"You won the toss, not the Nobel Prize," said Fox, and the umpire stifled a laugh.

All the players took up their positions and, as expected, Angelo 'The Glove' Blunt **picked up** Fox for the opening bounce. But Fox noticed that Angelo hadn't grown as much as Fox had over the past 12 months, and that he looked a little chunkier.

"Mmm, I might be able to run off him more easily this season," thought Fox.

Just at that moment, Angelo grabbed Fox's jumper and gave him a pinch.

"Then again, maybe not."

The Diggers' on-ball brigade consisted of Fox, Sammy, Rosie and Chung. They were up against Mace, the Glove, the former Roosters player Peter Rodan, and a new giant ruckman with flaming-red hair called 'Bluey'.

Before the umpire went to bounce the ball, Fox heard Rosie humming the *Bob the Builder* theme song as she walked past Mace.

"You are so dead!" said Mace furiously, going over

125

and giving Rosie a shove.

"Hey, cut that out!" said the umpire, throwing the ball to Rosie. "No. 7, your free kick."

Rosie quickly fired off a handball to Fox, who caught Angelo off guard as he flashed forward. He took two bounces and speared a perfect pass to Simon, who marked on the lead about 20 metres out, directly in front of goal.

The Dragons coach, Miles Winter, was furious. "Mace, you blockhead! Don't do that sort of thing while the umpire is looking!"

"But *Dad*!" whined Mace.

"But *Dad*!" mimicked Lewis from the boundary, causing everyone in the crowd to burst out laughing.

Simon lined up his shot and drilled the ball in between the two big sticks.

As the ball sailed through for a goal, a kookaburra started laughing.

"Shut up!" shouted Miles at the laughing bird.

| Dragons | 0.0 | (0) |
| Visitors | 1.0 | (6) |

Back in the centre, Chung went over to Mace and said, "Aw, you look really sad." And with a flick of his wrist, the young magician pulled a small bouquet of flowers from the sleeve of his jumper and offered it to Mace.

This infuriated Mace even further and he pushed

Chung over—right in front of the umpire.

"He doesn't have the ball—free kick to Diggers' No. 13!"

"What?!" cried Mace. "I hardly touched the wimp!"

While Mace argued with the umpire, Chung handballed to Rosie, who ran forward bouncing the football. She **drew an opponent,** then looped a handball over to Paige, who baulked around a Dragons defender and snapped a beautiful left-foot goal.

Once again the kookaburra started laughing.

"I said shut up!" Miles shouted at the bird.

Dragons	0.0	(0)
Visitors	2.0	(12)

Fox couldn't believe it—the Diggers had two goals on the board and the ball hadn't even been bounced yet!

But with Mace taking care to control his temper, the game soon tightened up. It was obvious that while the Diggers had the best eight or nine players on the ground, the rest of their team couldn't compete with the Dragons, who had very good players in every position. This meant

whenever a less talented Digger made a mistake, the Dragons would pounce—and more often than not it resulted in a goal.

The most embarrassing mistake came when Hugo once again completely misjudged the ball and it hit him in the head.

"Nice falcon, Trippitt!" yelled Mace. "You are such an unco loser!"

To make matters worse, after the ball had rebounded off Hugo's head it was picked up by Vince, who passed it to the Dragons' star full-forward, Sandy Barr. As Sandy kicked another goal for the Dragons, Mace yelled out, "Your goal, Trippitt!"

As the quarter progressed, Miles Winter became more and more upset with the kookaburra. It only ever seemed to laugh when the Diggers kicked a goal—when the Dragons scored there was a deathly silence.

"I'm going to kill that stupid bird!" said Miles through clenched teeth.

It was a **seesawing battle** and when the siren sounded for quarter-time the Diggers led by only one point.

Dragons   6.3 (39)
Visitors   6.4 (40)

During the break Mr Scott took off Mo, Rosie, Sammy and Simon. "You guys have been fantastic but we need to give everyone a go," he told them.

When Miles saw these star players heading to the bench at the start of the second quarter, he was thrilled.

"How pathetic is Greg Scott?" he sniggered. "What sort of idiot coach takes off some of his best players in a close game?"

Miles was still chuckling to himself over Mr Scott's stupidity when someone behind him growled, "Don't turn around!"

"What do you want?" asked Miles in a panic. Whoever it was behind him had a deep voice and sounded scary.

"I hear you have a little bird problem—maybe I can take care of it for you," said the stranger.

"You mean you'll get rid of that stupid kookaburra?"

"Yeah—ya want me to rub it out?"

"Really? Rub it out?"

Miles could not believe how lucky he was to have bumped into a "bird assassin" at a junior football match.

"Yes! I want you to rub it out," he replied enthusiastically. "I want it gone! Kaput! Never to be heard of again!"

"Turn around," the voice behind him commanded.

Miles spun around and was shocked to discover that the person standing behind him was none other than the young wildlife ranger, Bill Kelso.

"Mr Winter, do you realise it is a very serious offence to harm, or ask someone else to harm, a kookaburra?"

"Umm, I, errrr ..." stammered Miles.

"The answer is yes," said the ranger. "Now, I can either give you an on-the-spot fine or we can settle this matter in court …"

Miles could see the newspaper headlines if the matter went to trial: 'Kooky Coach Convicted Over Kookaburra Crime'.

"I'll pay the fine," he said quickly, pulling out his chequebook from his pocket.

"You can make the cheque out to 'The Wildlife Foundation' for … $5000."

"You have got to be kidding me—$5000?!"

"Okay then, see you in court …"

"No, no," said Miles. "I'll pay the fine."

He scribbled out the details and handed over the $5000 cheque to the ranger, who looked at it suspiciously.

"Hang on," said Bill, "this says 'Tilley Fawcett Inheritance Trust Account'."

"Don't worry about that—it's all above board," Miles said heartily. "Now I really must get back to coaching my team."

The second quarter was a good one for the Dragons. With a number of the Diggers' best players on the bench, the Dragons soon took the lead, and when the siren sounded for half-time they were up by 27 points.

Dragons   11.7 (73)
Visitors   7.4 (46)

Miles Winter was feeling much happier, and was even more thrilled when he discovered that Mr Scott was taking off Fox, Paige, Chris and Bruno for the third quarter.

"Fox Swift on the bench? Greg Scott is a born loser!" he thought to himself.

As expected, the Diggers sorely missed Fox and the other stars in the third quarter, and the margin blew out even further. At three-quarter time the scoreboard told a sorry tale.

| Dragons | 16.11 (107) |
| Visitors | 8.6 (54) |

With their best team on the field in the last quarter, the Diggers clicked into gear and came home strongly.

Fox dominated in the middle of the ground despite Angelo's **close-checking,** and Paige snapped three incredible goals in the final term that really lifted the team's spirits.

While many of the players tired in the last quarter, Fox was full of admiration for Rosie, who was running just as fast and hard as she had been at the start of the game.

The Diggers got the margin back to within 23 points with a few minutes to go and were making another push forward when Hugo once again misjudged the ball and was hit on the top of his head.

"Falcon!" yelled out Mace and Vince, roaring with laughter.

Unfortunately, Hugo's mistake ended up costing the Diggers a goal.

"That's the **sealer**, Dragons!" Miles yelled out arrogantly.

Lewis sprinted out to Hugo with a message from the coach.

"Mr Scott said not to worry about it, Hugo," he said. "Just make sure you watch the ball closely next time."

But Hugo still looked really down, so Lewis quickly added, "Hey, how do you make a tissue dance?"

"What?" asked Hugo.

"Put a little boogie in it!"

Hugo couldn't control his laughter—and neither could his opponent!

With the siren about to sound, and the Dragons 27 points ahead, Mace took a simple chest mark in the goalsquare.

"Oh, great," thought Fox. "Mace is going to kick a goal on the siren and really rub it in."

Mace slowly walked back to take his kick, trying to prolong his moment in the spotlight. He made sure his socks were pulled up and threw some grass into the air to check the direction of the breeze.

"Are you a footballer or a wind sock?" yelled out Lewis, causing everyone to laugh.

Mace glanced at the scoreboard.

Dragons	19.14 (128)
Visitors	15.9 (99)

"This will be our 20th," he thought as he started his run in.

But just as the Dragons' captain was about to send a drop punt through the big sticks, Gary the rabbit came from nowhere and ran in front of him.

Mace was so surprised by Gary's appearance that he completely miskicked the ball and it went sailing out of bounds on the full.

Everyone, including the Dragons players, burst out laughing.

"What's my stupid rabbit doing here?!" cried Mace.

"That's not your rabbit," said Chung. "It's *Fox's*."

"Say what?" said a furious Mace.

Mr Swift gave Paige, Simon, Rosie, Hugo, Mo and Lewis a lift home in his Kombi.

No one was speaking—they were all too upset about losing to the Dragons. Paige was particularly miserable and stared out the window, slowly shaking her head.

Paige was easily the most competitive athlete Fox had ever met. Even though she had played brilliantly and kicked five goals, she was still hurt by today's loss.

"It's not surprising that she's such a successful gymnast," thought Fox.

Mr Swift looked in the rear-view mirror and saw how gloomy Paige looked. He decided she needed cheering up and just at that moment one of his favourite songs came on the radio—*Happy* by Pharrell Williams. Mr Swift immediately started singing along, but he changed the words to make the song about Paige:

Listen closely to what I'm about to say
Paige Turner's here, she's a footy great
She's a dangerous typhoon,
with some awesome pace
She's got red hair and so much flair,
she always gets away
Because she's snappy
Snap a goal, if she feels there's a chance
to bang one through
Because she's snappy
Snap a goal with left or right,
her aim is always true
Because she's snappy
Snap a goal every week,
her opponents have no clue
Because she's snappy
Snap a goal, she's a star, as sure as cows go moo.

By now everyone in the car was splitting their sides laughing—even Paige couldn't stop herself from smiling.

Mr Swift continued to sing, with the Diggers providing the "yeahs".

Here comes Mace Winter saying this and that …
Yeah!
But you know our Paige she won't take no flak …
Yeah!
Paige loves to slot them from the boundary line
… Yeah!
I feel so sorry for Vince, when Paige kicks nine
Here's why …
Because she's snappy
Snap a goal, if she feels there's a chance to bang
one through
Because she's snappy
Snap a goal with left or right,
her aim is always true
Because she's snappy
Snap a goal every week,
her opponents have no clue
Because she's snappy
Snap a goal, she's a star, as sure as cows go moo.

Fox and his friends all knew the original song and they started clapping in time with the next section as Mr Swift kept singing.

Can't shut her down
Can't nothing … shut her down

Her skills are too good, can't shut her down
Can't nothing … shut her down
I said … tell ya about
The backmen all frown
Can't nothing … shut her down
Her goals are so fly … even off the ground
Can't nothing … shut her down

By now everyone knew the words of Mr Swift's version of the chorus, so they all joined in—including Paige!

I said …
Because she's snappy
Snap a goal, if she feels there's
a chance to bang one through
Because she's snappy
Snap a goal with left or right,
her aim is always true
Because she's snappy
Snap a goal every week,
her opponents
have no clue
Because she's snappy
Snap a goal, she's a star,
as sure as cows go moo.

WE ARE NOT
A - MOO - SED

Everyone sang the chorus again and this time they all let out a big

"Moooooo!" when it finished. By the time the song was over, Paige was laughing so hard she had tears rolling down her cheeks.

Mr Swift caught his son's eye in the rear-view mirror and gave him a wink. Fox smiled and winked back.

"As dads go, mine is pretty cool," thought Fox.

10

I Court
a Rabbit

Four days after the loss to the Dragons, Fox arrived home from school and collected the mail from the letterbox.

As usual he tossed the pile of envelopes on the small table just inside the front door for his parents to read later on.

He was about to look for Chase to see if he wanted to have a kick in the backyard when he noticed the envelope on the top of the pile had *his* name neatly typed on it.

"Mail for me? Cool!" thought Fox, who had never received a letter before.

He ripped open the envelope and quickly read the letter inside.

Francis Swift,

You are summoned to attend Davinal Community Court at 4pm on Friday 7 May to defend a charge made against you of stealing a white rabbit belonging to Mace Winter. You will be required to bring the aforementioned rabbit with you to the court and argue your case in front of Judge Trudy Binding.

"Uh-oh,' thought Fox.

Fox was nervous on the drive to court. And his brother was not helping the situation.

"Fox, if you go to jail can I have your footy?" asked Chase.

"Your brother is *not* going to jail," said Mrs Swift.

"Oh," sighed Chase.

"Don't sound so disappointed!" said Fox.

"Mum, how come I have to dress up in nice clothes when Fox is the criminal?" asked Chase.

"Your brother is *not* a criminal," said Mrs Swift.

"That's right—he's an *alleged* criminal," said Mr Swift.

"Gee, thanks, Dad," said Fox.

Fox looked across at Gary the rabbit, who was sitting happily in a small cardboard box next to Fox. Gary had voluntarily hopped into the green Kombi almost as if he wanted to go to court.

When they got there, Fox was happy to see a lot of his friends had turned up to support him. His best mate Lewis cheered him up by putting on a British accent and pretending to be a news reporter.

"And now arriving at the court are the Swift brothers ... Evil criminal masterminds or innocent victims? Either way, they look ridiculous wearing jackets and ties—unlike the star witness, Gary, who has scrubbed up beautifully for his big day in court!"

Fox laughed and said hello to his friends. As well as

Lewis, he could see Paige, Rosie, Simon, Chung and Hugo.

Hugo seemed distracted, and Fox noticed his friend was staring over at Bruno, who was talking to Hugo's sister Amanda.

"I might be going to jail, and you're more worried about your sister talking to Bruno?" Fox joked.

"Sorry, Fox," said Hugo. "Don't worry—my mind is now 100 per cent focused on you … Is Bruno holding my sister's hand?!"

Fox didn't have time to check, as he was being ushered through the doors by his parents.

The courtroom was a large chamber with about 30 rows of seats and wooden panelling on all the walls. At the front of the room was an impressive-looking bench, and Fox assumed this was where the judge would sit. He sat down in the front row, putting the box containing Gary on the seat beside him. The rest of his family sat directly behind him.

Fox sensed the room grow colder and turned around to see Miles Winter strutting down the middle aisle, with Mace following closely behind him.

Fox didn't think it was possible, but Mace had even more gel in his hair than usual. As did his father— though he didn't have much hair to put it on!

The Winters ignored Fox, but spoke loudly enough so that he could overhear them.

"This shouldn't take long, Mace—it's an open-and-shut case," Miles said confidently.

"Yep, we'll be home in time to have some rabbit pie for dinner," sneered Mace.

But their fun was interrupted when Judge Trudy suddenly swept into the room through the door next to the bench at the front.

"All rise for Judge Trudy Binding," said the tall clerk in a booming voice.

Everyone scrambled to their feet.

"Please be seated," bellowed the clerk once Judge Trudy had sat down.

Judge Trudy Binding had a reputation for being very strict, and those who entered her courtroom usually trembled in her presence. But there were two things Judge Trudy hated more than anything else: liars and people who wasted her time.

"Okay, let's get this show on the road," she said, examining some documents in front of her.

"What? A dispute about a rabbit? Seriously?!" she said, frowning at the two boys seated in the front row.

"Okay, so who owns the rabbit?" said Judge Trudy.

"I do," said Mace.

"And who is in possession of the rabbit?"

"I am," said Fox, pointing to the cardboard box beside him. "Gary kind of moved into our backyard."

Judge Trudy looked at Mace, then looked at his father.

"Then why are we in court? Why don't you just collect your rabbit instead of wasting my very valuable time?"

Miles rose and in his most professional legal voice said, "If it pleases Your Honour—"

"No, it does not please Your Honour!" snapped Judge Trudy.

"What I mean to say, Your Honour," said Miles, pointing at Fox, "is that this boy stole my son's precious rabbit and he should suffer the consequences."

Judge Trudy rolled her eyes and extended her right hand. "Okay, let's see the ownership papers."

Miles looked stunned. "The ... the ... ownership papers?"

"Yes, if it's your rabbit you'll need to prove it," said the judge.

Of course the Winters didn't have any ownership papers because Miles had taken the rabbit from Matilda Wall after evicting her while she was in a coma.

"Um, well, errr, you see ..."

"What *I see* is that you can't prove this is your rabbit—and so now I will need to decide who should get custody," said Judge Trudy. "And that is not an easy thing to do."

"I have a suggestion," said a voice sitting behind Mace.

Fox turned around and stared at the person who had dared to speak out of turn in Judge Trudy's courtroom. It was Vince.

"This had better be good, young man," said Judge Trudy.

"Thanks, Your Judgie-ness," said Vince, causing Mace to slap himself on the forehead. "Why don't you put the rabbit in between the two of them, and whoever the rabbit runs to can keep it."

Judge Trudy thought about this for a minute and said, "That's actually a pretty good idea. Okay, set it up and we will reconvene this hearing in 10 minutes."

She banged her gavel on the bench and swept out of the courtroom through the door behind her.

Vince smiled at Mace and said, "So am I a genius or what?"

"No, you are an *idiot*!" said Mace. "That rabbit hates me. Just because I yelled at it and tried to hit it with a stick."

"Don't worry," Vince said confidently, "I have a plan."

Mace looked at his father and they both shook their heads.

"We have lost this case for sure," thought Mace.

"I'll be back in a jiffy," said Vince. "I just need to grab something from the milk bar. Meet me in the alley next to the court in five minutes."

Five minutes later, in the alleyway, Vince handed Mace a bottle of carrot juice.

"What's that for?" asked Mace.

"I saw on TV that rabbits can't resist the smell of carrots," said Vince. "So all we have to do is pour carrot juice over your hands and that stupid rabbit will come hopping straight to you."

"You definitely saw this on TV?" said Mace a little uncertainly.

"Definitely," said Vince.

"Mmm, well, I suppose we have nothing to lose," said Mace, holding out his hands.

Vince poured the entire contents of the carrot juice bottle over his friend's hands, which caused them to turn slightly orange. The liquid also gave off a very carroty aroma. "Maybe this *will* work," thought Mace.

Back in the courtroom, the box containing Gary the rabbit was placed on the floor in front of Judge Trudy's bench.

Fox stood 3 metres to the left of the box and Mace stood 3 metres to the right.

"Okay boys, call the rabbit," commanded Judge Trudy.

Fox started calling out, "Gary, here Gary, come on Gary," while Mace simply waved his hands in the air so that the carroty smell would waft towards the rabbit.

The rabbit poked his head above the top of the box, his nostrils flaring as he sniffed the air. It took one look at Mace and bolted the other way straight into Fox's arms.

Judge Trudy announced, "I find that the rabbit belongs to Francis Swift until such time as someone comes forward with ownership papers that say otherwise. Court is now adjourned."

With that she banged her gavel on the bench and walked out, muttering, "Rabbits! What next?"

Fox was absolutely thrilled with the judge's decision, and his friends rushed over to congratulate him.

"I'm here with breaking news from the Davinal courthouse," said Lewis, continuing to impersonate an

English reporter, "where Fox Swift has just been found not guilty of rabbit rustling. We will now be bringing you an exclusive interview with Gary the rabbit—so Gary, how do you feel?"

Putting his imaginary microphone in front of Gary, Lewis then pretended to be Gary by speaking in a high-pitched voice out of the side of his mouth.

"I feel great, thanks, Lewis—I mean, imagine if I had to live with Mace? I'd rather live under Mr Grinter's armpit!"

"Oh gross!" said Paige and everyone laughed, which made Mace even angrier.

"So much for that idiotic carrot juice idea, Vince," he said. "Which stupid documentary said rabbits couldn't resist the smell of carrots?"

"Um, I think it was called something like *Doug's Bunny* ..."

"You mean *Bugs Bunny*?! Vince, you idiot—that's a cartoon!"

The next day, there was a large photo of Fox holding Gary the rabbit on the front page of the *Davinal Digest*. The headline above the photo was, 'Rabbit Catches a Fox'.

"That's a great photo," said Chase as the Swifts read the article together over breakfast.

"Thanks," said Fox.

"I meant of the rabbit!" laughed Chase.

Just then the doorbell sounded. "I'll get it!" Chase yelled out as he ran down the hallway.

After about 30 seconds, Chase reappeared in the kitchen. "There's an old lady at the door!" he announced at the top of his voice.

"Shhh, Chase!" said Mrs Swift. "That's not very polite."

"Sorry, Mum," said Chase. "… There's an old *person* at the door."

Mrs Swift shook her head and went to find out who was visiting them.

"Hi," she said when she reached the front door, "my name's Sasha Swift. How can I help you?"

The old woman held up the front page of the *Davinal Digest* and said, "Oh hello, dear. My name's Matilda Wall. I think you might have my rabbit."

Over a cup of tea, Matilda Wall explained how her rabbit had been stolen when she was in a coma at the local hospital.

"So let me get this straight," said Mrs Swift. "You're saying that Miles Winter evicted you for not paying your rent—while you were unconscious in hospital?"

Matilda Wall nodded sadly.

"That is an incredibly low act, even for Miles!" cried Mr Swift.

Matilda was staying at a friend's house a few kilometres away, and Mr Swift offered to drive her and Gary the rabbit there after they had finished hearing her story.

Fox came too, and was amazed to discover that the rabbit's name really was Gary, in honour of Matilda's late husband.

"I'll make sure Gary comes around to visit you, Fox—and he can still be a mascot for the Diggers," said Matilda.

As Mr Swift helped Matilda out of the van, he told her that she had been illegally evicted from her house by Miles and offered to represent her in court for free. Fox had never seen his dad so angry.

"So let me get this straight, Mr Winter," said Judge Trudy, sounding just like Mrs Swift. "You evicted Mrs Wall while she was in a *coma*—and then stole her rabbit?"

"Well, err, um, it was just a bit of a miscommunication," stammered Miles.

"Miscommunication?" mocked Judge Trudy. "How can someone who is unconscious communicate at all, let alone miscommunicate?!"

"Well, I, um ..."

"You will put Mrs Wall back into her accommodation

immediately," ordered the judge.

"Ahh, if only I could," said Miles. "Unfortunately that property now has a young family living in it, so I'm afraid my hands are tied."

"Well, you will have to offer Mrs Wall another of your properties," said the judge.

"More bad news there," said Miles, pretending to be really disappointed. "The only property I have vacant at the moment is a four-bedroom luxury house in Mayfair Street with a view of the river—and the rent there is sadly much more than Mrs Wall can afford to pay."

"I don't care! You will offer that four-bedroom house to Mrs Wall for the same rent she was paying you previously."

"But, but ... I'll lose so much money!" whined Miles.

"Oh, thanks for reminding me, Mr Winter—you will also be fined $10,000 for breaches of the real estate code," Judge Trudy said, banging her gavel on the bench to signify that the case was closed.

Matilda threw her arms around Mr Swift. "Thank you!" she said as the rest of the Swift family came over to congratulate her.

Miles Winter looked on in disgust.

"There is no justice!" he thought to himself. "And how am I supposed to pay this $10,000 fine?"

Then he remembered the Tilley Fawcett Inheritance Trust Account.

11

Young Guns

Lewis walked into class with giant bags under his eyes.

"Wow, Lewis, did you get *any* sleep last night?" asked Fox.

"Nope," said Lewis with a cheeky grin. "My cousins are down from Darwin for three weeks and we stayed up all night talking and laughing."

Mace and Vince entered the room and walked over to where Fox and Lewis were standing. Fox thought Mace would be a little more humble after his embarrassing attempt to attract Gary with the carrot juice. He was wrong.

"You are going down, Swift!" said Mace.

Quick as a flash, Fox turned to Vince. "Let me guess," he cut in as Vince was opening his mouth, "you're going to say, 'Yeah, you are *so* going down, Swift!'"

This put Vince on the spot—he had been about to

say exactly what Mace had said, but now he needed to come up with something of his own.

"You are so going … *up*, Swift!" he sneered triumphantly.

Fox and Lewis burst out laughing.

"Shut up, Vince," said Mace.

Lewis suddenly started sniffing the air. "Ah, what's up, Doc?" he said, imitating Bugs Bunny perfectly.

Mace quickly shoved his orange-tinted hands into his pockets and stormed off to his desk.

"Hey, that's pretty good!" said Vince enthusiastically. "Can you do Porky Pig?"

"Vince!" hissed Mace, and Vince quickly scuttled off to his desk.

At this point Mr Grinter arrived. He was only slightly late so he hoped Sally wouldn't make a note and pass it on to her father, as he had heard a rumour in the staff room that Mr Renton was considering sacking him.

Right at that moment, however, the principal had other things on his mind. Miles Winter was in his office, and that was rarely an enjoyable experience.

"So, Clive," said Miles in his most charming voice, "how's the wife?"

"Penny's well, thanks," said the principal. "She's excited I've finally been able to grow some apples, and she can't wait to start making apple pies!"

Mr Renton smiled as he thought about the huge shiny apples that were hanging from the tree outside his office. Mr Percy was a miracle worker!

"We must have you two around for dinner soon," said Miles.

"That sounds like a lot of fun," said Mr Renton, who couldn't think of anything worse.

Miles pointed to a tall bookcase behind Mr Renton and said, "What's that book on the top shelf?"

"Which one?" said Mr Renton, getting up from his chair to take a look.

"The one up on the far left—I'd really like to read it."

Mr Renton hopped up on a small ladder and attempted to retrieve the book that Miles had pointed out. Meanwhile, Miles sneakily left his chair and pinched a key that was hanging on a hook near the door. The key, which was labelled "Master Key", was able to open all the locks at Davinal Primary.

By the time Mr Renton had retrieved the book and hopped down off the ladder, Miles was back in his chair looking as innocent as possible.

The principal inspected the book, which was called *A Beginner's Guide to Dressmaking*.

"Why do you want to read a book about dressmaking, Miles?"

"Um, well, err … Excuse me, Clive, can I use your

private bathroom? I'll be back in a jiffy," said Miles, blushing bright red.

Right at that moment, back in Mr Grinter's classroom, Mace put up his hand.

"Sir, can I go to the toilet?" he said.

"Ooh, can I go too?" asked Vince.

A minute later, Mace and Vince were outside hiding in the bushes by the principal's bathroom window. Sticking his arm out the window, Miles passed them the master key. Then he returned to Mr Renton's office to continue the discussion about dressmaking.

After five awkward minutes of conversation, Miles suddenly clutched his stomach and said, "Sorry, Clive, I need to use your toilet again—I really must get Mrs Winter to stop making so much curry!"

Miles went back into the principal's bathroom and opened the window.

"How did you go?" he whispered as he took the master key back from Mace and Vince, who were once again hiding in the bushes.

"All done," Mace said proudly.

"Excellent work," said Miles, closing the window and returning to the principal's office once more.

"There's another book I'd like to read up there on the top shelf," said Miles as he entered the room. "Would

153

you mind getting it down for me, Clive?"

As Mr Renton climbed back up on the ladder, Miles quickly returned the master key to its hook.

The principal looked at the cover of the book before handing it to Miles. "*Hip-Hop Dancing Made Easy*?" he asked, raising an eyebrow.

"Mmm, yes, I've always wanted to hop-hip."

"Hip-hop?"

"Either way," said Miles, who was totally clueless about dancing. "Well, I'd better get going—will you walk me out to my car, Clive?" he said, quickly changing the subject.

"Sure," said Mr Renton. "Ooh, don't forget your dressmaking book!"

"Ah … thanks," said Miles.

As they walked out of the building, Mr Renton stopped suddenly.

"What's the matter?" said Miles innocently.

The principal was staring at his precious apple tree in horror.

"My apples!" he cried. "Someone has stolen my apples!"

And sure enough, where there had been seven giant, juicy apples on the tree, now only one remained.

"That's shocking!" said Miles. "I wonder which students could have possibly done this?"

"You think some students stole my apples?" said Mr Renton.

"Well, who else could it have been?" said Miles. "But they can't have got far—they would have had to stash the apples somewhere safe until the heat died down. Hmm, I don't know—in their lockers, maybe? It's a pity you aren't able to open all the lockers and find out who did this."

"But I *can* open all the lockers," said Mr Renton triumphantly. "I have a master key!"

"Of course," said Miles, a sly smile creeping across his face. "Why didn't I think of that?"

"I tell you, Miles, when I find the culprits, they will be getting three Friday detentions for this!" said a furious Mr Renton.

"You are going too easy on them, Clive," said Miles. "For something this serious, I'd teach whoever it was a lesson they'd never forget by giving them three *Saturday* detentions!"

Mr Renton stomped off, grabbed the master key from the hook in his office and set about opening each student's locker.

Half an hour later the principal burst into Mr Grinter's classroom in a rage.

Mr Grinter was sound asleep with his head on his desk in a pool of drool at the time, but Mr Renton was so angry he didn't care.

"The following students will have detention each Saturday morning for the next three weeks," he barked furiously. "Paige Turner, Bruno Gallucci, Simon Wallace, Chung Lee, Rosie McHusky and Fox Swift."

"What for?" said Fox.

"For stealing my apples!" roared the headmaster.

"But we didn't!" said Fox.

"Then how did each of you come to have one of my apples in your locker?"

The six friends sat in stunned silence. None of them had any idea how the principal's precious apples could have ended up in their lockers.

"So," Mr Renton continued, still fuming, "for the next three Saturday mornings, you will all be in detention. And Mr Grinter, *you* will be in charge!"

Before Mr Grinter had time to object, Mr Renton turned and stormed out of the classroom.

"Looks like the Diggers are going to lose their next three matches," said Mace, with an evil smirk.

"Yeah—with six of your best players out, there's no way you losers can win," crowed Vince as he and Mace high-fived.

At lunchtime, Fox chatted to his mates about this disastrous turn of events.

"I don't know how he did it, but Mace is definitely behind this," he said.

All his friends were looking miserable, but Hugo

looked the most upset of any of them.

"Hey Hugo, don't look so down," said Fox. "At least *you* can still play."

"There were seven apples on that tree, but they didn't even bother to frame me," said Hugo sadly. "Because I'm not a threat."

The first Saturday detention was the longest three hours of Fox's life. Paige, Simon, Bruno, Rosie and Chung were also in gloomy moods.

The Diggers were playing the Stonewarren Stingrays, who had made the finals last year, and for the first time in his life Fox agreed with Vince—there was no way his team could win.

To make matters worse, Mr Grinter snored loudly throughout the detention while Fox and his friends wrote out "I must not steal the principal's apples" over and over.

When the detention finished, Fox suggested they all go around to Mr Scott's place to cheer him up.

"He's probably going to be pretty upset," he said. "This will be two losses in a row."

They arrived at Mr Scott's house and knocked on the door. Their coach answered with a beaming smile.

"Hey! Great to see you guys—come on in!"

"Wow," thought Fox, "he's taking the loss really well."

Fox and his friends filed inside and sat down in Mr Scott's lounge room looking miserable.

"How come you all look so sad?" asked Mr Scott.

"We feel like we let you down," said Paige.

"Yeah, even though we didn't steal the apples, we feel like the loss today was our fault," said Simon.

"The loss?" said Mr Scott. "You guys haven't heard?"

"Haven't heard what?" said Bruno.

"We won! We won by 15 points!"

"What?! I mean, great! I mean, how?!" stammered Fox.

As Mr Scott explained what had happened, Fox's mouth opened wider and wider.

"Thankfully, just before the game we picked up five new recruits," said Mr Scott.

"Wow!" said Chung. "Who were they?"

"Chase Swift, Jimmy Rioli and three of Jimmy's cousins who were visiting from Darwin—"

"Wait a minute!" interrupted Fox. "Chase and Jimmy played?!"

"*Played*? They starred!" cried Mr Scott. "There was one time when Chase picked up the ball in the back pocket and then he and Jimmy handballed to each other all the way down the field until Chase snapped a goal. It was a-mazing!"

Fox was too stunned to speak. Chase hadn't said a word to him about signing up to play for the Diggers.

"And Jimmy's cousins are *so* skilful—they played in

bare feet, just like they do back in the Tiwi Islands!" added Mr Scott.

Fox had never been prouder of his brother. Chase was half the size of some of the Stonewarren Stingrays, but that hadn't stopped him from wanting to help out the Diggers.

The six friends began jumping around their coach's lounge room, high-fiving each other and screaming out "Wooo!" and "Yessss!" at the top of their lungs.

The next morning Miles Winter was sitting at his kitchen table. He was wearing his silk dressing gown with the initials "MW" on the pocket, and a shower cap. He was wearing the shower cap because he had just rubbed hair-regrowth cream into his scalp. For

reasons known only to himself, he continued to use this cream every day despite the fact that no new hair had grown for more than 20 years.

Miles added his sixth teaspoon of sugar to his coffee and picked up the newspaper. He was looking forward to reading all about the Diggers' loss to the Stonewarren Stingrays, but his eyes widened as he read the results.

When he saw the name "Swift" mentioned in both the best players and goalkickers, he exploded.

"Fox Swift was supposed to be in detention! That dirty cheat!"

He looked at the results again and saw the name "Rioli". "What? How can Lewis Rioli be in the best players? He's hopeless!"

"Mace!" yelled out Miles. "What is going on?!"

When Miles discovered that it was Chase and Jimmy who had played and starred for the Diggers, he was furious. He decided to go the Junior Football Tribunal and attempt to have them banned from playing because they were too young.

Hugo had outsmarted Miles at several previous Tribunal hearings, and Miles was determined to win this time. Fortunately for him, the Tribunal chairman this year was a man named Robin Graft, who was open to taking bribes.

Miles rang Robin and said, "If I give you $1000, will you make sure I win?"

"No!" said Mr Graft. "But for $2000 I will."

Miles smiled as he wrote out yet another cheque from the Tilley Fawcett Inheritance Trust Account.

The only flaw in his plan was that he talked about it with Mace, who in turn told Vince.

At school on the day of the Tribunal hearing, Vince was teasing Chung at lunchtime.

"Bad luck about Chase and Jimmy," he sneered.

"What do you mean?" said Chung. "We don't find out whether they're allowed to play again until tonight."

"Ha! Robin Graft is going to say whatever Mr Winter wants him to say," said Vince. "All he has to do is turn up and it's game over for Jimmy and Chase."

That night, just as Mr Graft was about to leave for the Tribunal, there was a knock on his door. When he opened it, he was surprised to see a young Asian boy standing there.

"Hi there," said Chung. "My dog's gone missing and I think he might be in your backyard."

"Sorry, kid," said Mr Graft. "I have to go to an important meeting now, so I haven't got time to check. Goodbye."

With that, he walked outside, pulling the door closed

behind him with a loud snap. Mr Graft then sidestepped Chung and walked briskly towards his car.

He reached into his pocket for his car keys and was surprised to find it was empty.

"Darn! Must have left them inside," he said to himself as he hurried back towards his front door. He reached into his other pocket, where he always kept his house keys, only to discover that it too was empty. He was locked out of his house and his car.

"This is a disaster!" Mr Graft said to himself. "I'd better ring Miles and tell him I won't be able to make it to the Tribunal hearing."

He had taken his phone out from the inner pocket of his coat and was halfway through dialling Miles' number when he realised he was holding the remote control for his TV.

"How the heck ... ?" he said, before throwing the remote control at the door with a cry of frustration.

If he hadn't been making such a fuss, he might just have heard Chung giggling in the bushes nearby.

Miles kept looking at his watch as he waited nervously for Robin Graft to arrive at the Tribunal hearing.

"Looks like we'll have to postpone the hearing," he said to Hugo.

"Not necessarily," said Hugo. "According to the rules, if the chairman of the Tribunal is unable to appear, then the assistant chairman can stand in for them."

"And, um, who is the assistant chairman?" asked Miles.

"Mabel Hurley," said Hugo, with a grin.

Miles went as white as a ghost.

Mabel 'Hannibal' Hurley was the local driving instructor. Not only was she impossible to bribe, but she also couldn't stand Miles.

"Okay, let's get cracking," barked Mabel as she marched in. "Who is prosecuting this case?"

"I am," squeaked Miles, standing up.

Mabel noticed that he was wearing a barrister's wig on his head, and rolled her eyes. "Is this guy for real?!" she thought.

Miles was trembling so much he didn't even notice when Lewis, who was sitting directly behind him, slipped a small device into his side pocket.

"The first thing I want to say is this—" began Miles, clearing his throat. But his speech was interrupted by a long, loud farting noise—and it seemed to be coming from Miles himself.

Everyone roared with laughter.

"Mr Winter, please control yourself!" cried Mabel in disgust.

"That wasn't me!" said Miles, but no one believed him.

He cleared his throat again and tried to continue. "My case is built on the following argument—" but Lewis hit the button again.

Ppllllrrrffff!

This was followed by more laughter, and another awkward pause from Miles.

"As I was saying, we can't have young children playing against older kids because—"

Ppllllrrrffff!

"That's not me!" cried Miles. "It can't be—I take anti-flatulence tablets every day!" But this just caused everyone to laugh even louder.

"In conclusion, I believe that the Tribunal has a duty to—"

Ppllllrrrffff!

No one was able to hear Miles' final remarks, because they were all laughing too hard.

As Miles sat down, Lewis gave the button one last push. Mabel Hurley screwed up her nose in disgust.

It was time for the Diggers to state their case, and Hugo rose to his feet. "I call Chase Swift and Jimmy Rioli to the witness stand," he said, with a sense of drama.

Mabel frowned and cleared her throat, "We don't actually have a witness stand, Hugo."

"Um, okay—I call them to the front of the room then."

Chase and Jimmy made their way to the front, and Hugo clasped his hands behind his back and started walking back and forth, just like he'd seen the lawyers do on TV.

"Is it true you two boys played for an under-13s team on the weekend?" he said.

"Yes," said Jimmy and Chase together.

"And how old are you?" asked Hugo.

"Nine," came the joint reply.

"And is nine *under* 13?"

"Yes."

"In that case, Mrs Hurley," said Hugo, turning his attention to the assistant chairman, "surely these boys are eligible to play? Otherwise they should have called the competition: 'the under-13-*and-over-11s*'."

Mabel Hurley looked at Miles and said, "The kid's right. Chase and Jimmy are allowed to play for the

Diggers. Case dismissed."

Miles shot to his feet to argue, but as he stood up there was another *Ppllllrrrfff* sound. He quickly sat back down.

"Maybe next time you should employ Hugo to argue your case, Mr Winter," whispered Lewis.

12

Night of Talent

Miles Winter was in a very bad mood when he left the Tribunal. He was so busy muttering furiously to himself that he didn't pay attention to where he was going and walked straight into Chung Lee's father, Feng.

"Hey, watch where you're going!" yelled Miles.

"Oh, I am sorry," said Feng, "but as a matter of fact it was you who walked into me—"

"I did not!" snapped Mr Winter. "And when are you going to get a job and stop mooching off our government?"

"Well, I—" began Mr Lee, who wasn't in fact receiving any money from the Australian government whatsoever.

"Oh, go open a Chinese restaurant," Mr Winter said rudely, in the tone of telling someone to go jump in a lake, and then stalked off into the night.

Mr Lee smiled. Miles Winter had just given him an

idea. He went home, logged on to his computer, and started researching Chinese restaurants in the district—the closest one was 147 kilometres away.

After all, Feng had come down under for a change of pace—and running a nice, quiet little restaurant in country Australia was about as far from being a nuclear scientist in a busy city as you could get.

He and his wife, Ting, also had a real passion for cooking—they loved spending time together in the kitchen, trying new recipes and making their own adjustments to old family favourites. Mr Lee's experiments didn't always pay off, but Mrs Lee was an amazing cook, and she thought opening a restaurant was a fantastic idea.

All they needed was to borrow some money to help start the business, so Mr Lee made an appointment to see Mr Shloogal at the Davinal Bank.

Unfortunately, Mr Shloogal told the Lees they would need at least $25,000 in the bank before he would lend them any money.

"But if I had $25,000 in the bank I wouldn't need to borrow any money!" said Mr Lee.

Chung told Fox about his dad's problem and Fox decided to do something about it. At the end of footy training he called the team together in the changing rooms.

"Hey everyone, listen up! Chung's parents want to

open a Chinese restaurant in Davinal and I reckon that's pretty cool. If anyone has any suggestions on how we can raise some money to help them get started, please let me know."

There was silence as Fox's teammates tried to come up with ideas.

"Wydonwehav'nitotalen?" mumbled Mo Officer.

"Mo, that's a brilliant idea," cried Paige. "A night of talent!"

Everyone became very excited by this idea and immediately started coming up with different activities that could help make the night a success.

"We could get people to donate items and sell them off," suggested Rosie, who had been involved in fundraisers for her athletic clubs in the past.

"Lots of us could do acts," said Simon. "Like Chung could do magic and someone else could sing a song—"

"We'll need lots of people to turn up—maybe Shazza and Bazza could promote the night on their local radio show?" said Hugo.

"I could draw pictures of people as they arrive and sell them," said Lewis.

"And Lewis, you *have* to host the night—that would be a ripper!" said Chung.

Fox smiled as he watched his teammates brainstorming plans for the night.

As soon as he arrived home after training, Fox told his

parents about the proposed Diggers "Night of Talent".

"That's fantastic, Fox! I'll see if I can book the town hall—the mayor owes me a favour," said Mr Swift.

"And I can invite some of our lawyer friends from the city—they love to support a good cause," Mrs Swift added enthusiastically.

"This is really going to happen!" thought Fox excitedly. "I wonder if we can raise a thousand dollars?"

"They'll be lucky to raise 50 cents!" said Miles Winter when Mace and Vince told him about the Night of Talent at training two days later. "Who's going to turn up to watch a bunch of talentless kids making complete idiots of themselves?"

"Actually I wouldn't mind going," said Vince, "Apparently Chung is doing some magic tricks, and he's really good—"

Miles and Mace both gave Vince death stares.

"—but as if I'd *ever* go," he finished quickly.

Fox had thought of two ways he could help with the night. The first involved visiting the local printing shop called 'Bigg Print', which was owned by a friendly man called Jamie Bigg. Fox introduced himself to Mr Bigg, who was in fact very small, and explained about the Night of Talent. Mr Bigg agreed to help out by designing an invitation that could be put in people's letterboxes or sent out by email—and even offered to do it for free.

Fox also sent an email to Cyril Rioli to see if he had any ideas for items they could auction off on the night. Cyril replied straight away saying he could organise two donations: the first was a Hawthorn jumper signed by all the players at the club; the second was two tickets to a Hawks game—and whoever bought them could go into the Hawthorn changing rooms after the game.

"No way!" thought Fox. "That is the most amazing auction item ever."

A few days later, Fox was in the Kombi with his dad listening to Bazza and Shazza's radio program.

Bazza: "And coming up next Saturday evening is the Davinal Diggers' Night of Talent, which is going to be an absolute rip-snorter, Shazza!"

Shazza: "It'll certainly be a bigger hit than that beard you're trying to grow, Bazza. In fact there are only 22 spots still available—and the town hall seats nearly 500!"

Bazza: "My beard is way cool, Shazza ... and speaking of cool, I am seriously digging the invitations to this Night of Talent—way to go, Mr Bigg! And get this, Shazza—I heard a little rumour that one Cyril Rioli might be making an appearance!"

Shazza: "Hold on to your hat, Bazza, because I've

just received a text from the town hall and the event is now completely sold out!"

"Woohoo!" cried Fox, high-fiving his dad.

The town hall looked amazing for the Diggers' Night of Talent. The players had spent hours setting up blue and yellow decorations and even the serviettes on the tables were in the Diggers' colours.

Men and women piled into the town hall and took their places at the 50 tables.

"With 10 people at each table and tickets costing $20 each, that means …" Fox furrowed his brow as he tried to work out how much money that was.

"Yep, $10,000," Hugo said casually, as if reading his mind.

"Oh my God!" said Fox out loud.

Fox waved to his parents. Sitting with Cyril Rioli at their table was a bunch of their legal friends from the city, including the famous barrister Julian Fireside.

Lewis took to the stage with a microphone in his hand. He didn't look at all nervous, despite the fact that there were 500 people in the audience.

"Wow, there are *so* many people here! That rumour I started about Katy Perry and P!nk performing tonight has really paid off!"

Everyone started laughing, and straight away Lewis had the audience in the palm of his hand. He pointed out the treadmill on the side of the stage, and invited Rosie McHusky to hop on to it.

"Rosie McHusky is going to run a half-marathon on that treadmill tonight. That's right—she's going to run 21.1 kilometres and you can sponsor her per kilometre. Just fill in the sponsorship forms on your table, and Rosie will do the rest. Let's give Rosie a huge cheer as she sets off on her epic journey!"

The audience burst into applause as Rosie started running on the treadmill, and people immediately started filling in the sponsorship forms on their tables.

Lewis then introduced the acts one at a time, and they all received a fantastic response.

First up was Chung, performing a series of magic tricks. He was joined on stage by his two furry assistants, and Fox loved it when he managed to pull Gary the rabbit out of a hat. He also kept making objects appear in Joey's pouch. Lewis then introduced 'Maths-Boy' to the stage—it was Hugo,

173

dressed as a giant calculator.

Hugo started off by asking people to yell out a number of goals and points, promising to tell them the total score on the spot.

A man near the front immediately yelled out, "A hundred and sixty-seven goals and 96 points."

"One thousand and ninety-eight," Hugo said without missing a beat.

This impressed everyone, and the numbers quickly got bigger and bigger until someone eventually called out, "What about 66,742 goals and 3702 points?"

"That's 404,154," said Hugo as quick as a flash.

He received a standing ovation for that one.

Fox and Chase came on stage and performed footy tricks. They rolled balls down their arms and behind their necks, then kicked and handballed footies through a basketball hoop with pinpoint accuracy.

Without a doubt the most surprising act was Mo Officer. Fox couldn't believe how someone who spoke with such an impossible mumble could have such a clear and pure singing voice. He sang a song by his favourite country and western singer, Johnny Cash, called *I Walk the Line*, and some members of the audience were so moved they started to cry!

Paige had the crowd gasping by performing a series of spectacular gymnastic moves, including somersaults and cartwheels.

The biggest crowd-pleaser was when Bruno performed a duet with Hugo's sister Amanda. Bruno looked really cool with his hair slicked back and Amanda looked stunning as they danced and sang their way through *You're the One that I Want* from an old film called *Grease*. Everyone stood up and clapped along—except for Hugo, who didn't know where to look.

After the performances, Lewis auctioned off the items that had been donated by generous supporters. Fox's favourite item was Joey's Diggers jumper, which she had worn to the previous year's Grand Final. Mo and Snowy Davison—the pensioner who had taught the Winters a lesson that year and was now a passionate Diggers supporter—had mounted the jumper in a big frame and Joey had "signed" it with a paw print.

Julian Fireside purchased Cyril's donation of Hawthorn tickets and a visit to the Hawthorn rooms for a whopping $5000. He then gave those tickets to Chris and Sammy, and promised to introduce them to his good friend Nic Naitanui! Chris and Sammy smiled, laughed and danced for the rest of the evening.

But the auction item that received the most interest was the final one that Lewis announced.

"Okay, to finish off the night I have something for the *ladies*! Yes, you asked for it and you got it—the final auction item tonight is … a date with the Diggers' very own coach, Mr Scott!"

When Mr Scott walked out on stage, the audience initially fell silent. The man standing next to Lewis didn't resemble the old Mr Scott at all. That afternoon the Diggers' coach had visited a local beauty salon, where a man named 'Pierre Pierre' had given him a complete makeover. He was given a trendy haircut and his 1970s sideburns were removed, his nails were manicured, his nostril hairs were trimmed and he was decked out in a really cool outfit. He looked fantastic.

Suddenly everyone started whooping and hollering.

"Oh my God!" said Paige. "Mr Scott looks just like George Clooney!"

"Let the bidding begin!" said Lewis.

It soon became a bidding war between two wealthy local women.

"One thousand dollars!" cried Annabelle Granger.

"Fifteen hundred!" yelled Cynthia Millington.

"Two thousand!" responded Annabelle Granger.

Joey couldn't watch and put her paws over her eyes. Mr Scott was quite scared of both Annabelle and Cynthia and didn't really want either of them to win. "It's for a good cause," he reminded himself.

"The bid from Annabelle Granger is now $3500. Miss Millington, it's back to you," said Lewis.

Cynthia Millington angrily folded her arms to indicate she was no longer bidding, and Annabelle Granger smiled smugly.

"Three thousand five hundred going once ... $3500 going twice ..."

Mr Scott felt a knot in his stomach. He did not want to go on a date with Annabelle Granger.

"Three thousand five hundred going for a third and final t—"

"Five thousand!" called out a woman's voice.

The audience gasped as one, then heads turned to find out the identity of this mystery bidder.

The woman was sitting on Fox's parents' table. Her name was Samantha Lu and she was strikingly beautiful.

"Back to you, Miss Granger," said Lewis. "Five thousand dollars going once, going twice ..."

"Come on, Cynthia," said Annabelle Granger. "As if we'd want a date with Greg Scott anyway." And with that, the two women stood up and walked out hand-in-hand with their noses in the air.

Lewis called Mr Scott over and said, "Five thousand dollars! What do you think of that?"

After a long pause, all Mr Scott could say was, "Wow!"

"Thankfully he's a much better talker when he's coaching the Diggers!" said Lewis.

Mrs Swift dashed up on to the stage and handed Lewis a piece of paper with the latest fundraising figures.

"Woah!" said Lewis. "After we add the $2250 raised by the incredible Rosie McHusky, the total amount of money collected is … $35,550!"

At these words the audience went wild.

"To finish up, I would like to ask Mr Lee to come up on stage and say a few words."

Mr Lee took the microphone from Lewis and wiped a tear from his eye.

"I promised my wife I wouldn't cry," he said, "and clearly I have already broken that promise. On behalf of my family, thank you all so much. I promise that our new restaurant, which will be called 'Feng's Way', will be, as you say here, 'a bloody ripper'—and that's a promise we *will* keep. Finally, I really want to thank the Diggers Football Club—I hope they beat the Dragons in the Grand Final!"

The audience went wild once again and Mr Lee wiped away a few more tears.

Fox went over to his parents' table, where Mr Scott

was talking to Samantha Lu.

"You don't have to go on a date with me if you don't want to," said Samantha. "If you'd prefer it, I can just donate the money—"

"No, no," insisted a clearly smitten Mr Scott. "I think legally we *have* to go on a date."

Fox smiled. The Diggers' Night of Talent had been a success beyond his wildest dreams.

From there things happened amazingly quickly for the Lee family. Mr Lee got his loan from the bank and the owner of a restaurant on Main Street who was looking to retire offered to sell them his business. Feng's Way had its official opening a fortnight later, and thanks to the publicity from the Night of Talent, it was flooded with bookings. Everyone in Davinal seemed thrilled they were finally getting a Chinese restaurant—except for Miles Winter, who was furious.

"How come you're so angry about Mr Lee opening his restaurant?" said Vince after the next Dragons training session.

"It starts with a Chinese restaurant, then what next?" said Miles. "All of a sudden there'll be a Sudanese restaurant and then a Vietnamese restaurant and soon enough there's no room for a good old-fashioned, fair dinkum Aussie pizza place!"

"But aren't pizzas Italian?" asked Vince.

"Well, um, sort of. It's just, you know … Vince, you're too young to understand."

Miles had worked out a plan to make sure Feng Lee's restaurant would fail. It was simple, but ingenious in an evil kind of way. On the opening night he would get Mace and Vince to release rats in the restaurant, and after that no one would ever want to eat there again.

To make matters even worse, Miles made sure there would be two special guests dining at Feng's Way on the opening night. The first was a famous food critic called Pat Meston. Pat was a popular TV personality who always wore a colourful bow tie. If Pat Meston wrote a bad review about a restaurant, that restaurant struggled to survive. And if Pat Meston saw a rat in a restaurant, he would definitely write a terrible review.

The second special guest was the local health inspector, Mr Fink. Mr Fink—who looked rather rat-like himself, with his sharp features and slight buckteeth—took public-health risks very seriously. He was known to close shops and restaurants if he found even a hint of rat poo, let alone an actual rat.

"He will definitely close down Feng's Way after he sees a plague of rats running through the place!" thought Miles, with a smile.

As the excited guests arrived at Feng's Way on the opening night, they were greeted by Feng Lee himself. Fox and his Diggers friends were also there, lending a hand by serving tables and washing dishes.

Pat Meston wore a bright-green and orange bow tie, and he asked Mr Lee lots of tricky questions about the menu. But Mr Lee was able to answer them all, and Pat Meston nodded with approval. Nearby sat Mr Fink, his eyes constantly darting around as he sniffed the air.

Everything was going beautifully—the food Mrs Lee had prepared was superb, the Diggers players were doing a great job bringing out the meals and clearing tables, and the guests were all laughing and having a fantastic night.

That was when Mace snuck in the back door of the restaurant with Vince, who was carrying a brown hessian sack. Whatever was inside was moving and squeaking.

"Vince, when I open this door, you let out the rats, okay?" said Mace.

"Can you give me a one, two, three countdown?" asked Vince.

Mace rolled his eyes. "Yes! I'll give you a one, two, three!"

"Great. Oh Mace, are you going to say one, two, three—*go?*"

"What?"

"I just want to know whether I let the rats out on 'three' or on 'go'?"

"Shut up, Vince! Just go!"

Hearing voices, Fox looked over to the door near the back of the restaurant and saw Mace and Vince emptying out something from a brown sack.

"Rats!" he thought in alarm.

It was too late to stop the rats from being released, and he knew if the diners saw them it would be a disaster. Thinking quickly, he grabbed Lewis. "We need a diversion," he whispered. "Mace and Vince have just dumped some rats at the back of the room, so we need you to distract everyone while the rest of us grab the rats before anyone spots them!"

Fox knew the only person in the world who would not be flustered by this request was Lewis. "He'll think of something," he thought confidently.

And he was right—Lewis went to the front of the restaurant, cleared his throat and made an announcement: "Ladies and gentlemen, welcome to Feng's Way. In honour of the opening night, I have written a special rap song that I'd like to share with you."

Everyone started clapping.

Lewis spotted Miss Carey eating alone on a table nearby. This gave him an idea.

"And I'd like to ask Miss Scarey—" he began.

"It's Miss *Carey*!" interrupted the principal's assistant.

"Sorry—I'd like to ask *Miss Carey* to provide me with the beat."

Everyone was quite surprised when the prim and proper Miss Carey started busting out a fairly reasonable beat for Lewis to build his rap around.

Meanwhile Fox, Paige, Simon, Rosie, Chung, Bruno and Hugo were frantically trying to catch all the rats and put them into bags. Fortunately all the diners had their eyes glued on Lewis and had no idea of the commotion that was taking place behind them.

"I call this one *The Feng's Way Rap*," said Lewis.

Davinal was missing a whole lotta flair
As sure as Mr Winter is losing all his hair
I said it out loud, didn't want to be rude
But what this town needs is some quality
Chinese food!

Everyone in the restaurant laughed and started clapping along.

Then along came Feng and his wife called Ting
Their food's so good it should be wearing bling!
If you wanna spring roll there's just one thing to say
Get off your butt and get to Feng's Way!
The dumplings are awesome
And the chicken's got some spice
If you want to send your tongue to heaven
Try Ting's Special Fried Rice!

When the last rat had been collected, Fox whispered something to Paige and Simon and they shot out the door with the rat-filled bags. He then gave Lewis the thumbs up.

Thank you for attending
on dis special opening night
You're a good-looking crowd—you guys
are dyno-mite!
When you leave later,
make sure you tell your mates
That as restaurants go,
this is one of the all-time greats!

The diners all gave Lewis a standing ovation and food critic Pat Meston made a note about the excellent entertainment provided at Feng's Way.

Fox and Hugo then casually walked over to where Mr Fink was sitting.

"Have you heard the news?" Fox asked Hugo in a slightly raised voice.

"No, what's going on?" said Hugo.

"Apparently there's a rat plague at the Dragons' football ground."

"That's not good with all those kids playing footy there!" exclaimed Hugo.

Fox noticed something moving out of the corner of his eye—it was Mr Fink putting some money for his dinner on the table and bolting for the door.

Fox and Hugo high-fived as they watched him jump into his car and screech away from the kerb on his way to the Dragons' football ground.

Of course, that was precisely where Fox had instructed Paige and Simon to drop off the rats!

The next morning Miles Winter was sitting at the breakfast table wearing his silk pyjamas and shower cap. Remembering his recent humiliation at the Tribunal, he swallowed an extra three anti-flatulence tablets.

Miles was really looking forward to reading the newspaper. He had quickly scanned the front page of the *Davinal Digest* and spotted two large headlines— one mentioned a restaurant opening and the other a rat plague.

"Oooh, this is going to be *so* sweet," he thought. "Bye bye, Feng!"

But as Miles read the articles more closely, he turned purple with anger.

The first article gave a glowing review of Davinal's new restaurant. "Feng's Way was well worth the four-hour drive from the city," Pat Meston had written. "This place will become an institution in Davinal—it is a slice of China that is here to stay!"

"Noooooooooooooo!" thought Miles.

His horrible plan had failed. "At least things can't get any worse," he thought.

He was wrong.

The other article on the front page was a report about a plague of rats that had been uncovered at the Dragons Junior Football Club. The health inspector, Mr Fink, was quoted as saying that the club would face a substantial fine.

"Okay, *now* things can't get any worse," thought Miles.

But he was wrong again.

Right then his phone started ringing—and it didn't stop ringing for the next hour and a half. The parents of his expensive recruits all called him to demand more money as compensation for their boys playing at a rat-infested football club.

Miles went to his study, pulled out the Tilley Fawcett

Inheritance Trust Account chequebook and started writing cheques. Lots of cheques.

13

Over the Rainbow

ox, Bruno, Rosie, Paige, Chung and Simon all sat watching the clock as it ticked down to the end of their third and final Saturday detention. The second it was over, the six Diggers players raced from the classroom into the brilliant sunshine, leaving Mr Grinter sound asleep at his desk.

As soon as Fox got home he went straight to Chase's room to find out if the Diggers had won.

As usual, Chase was so excited he blurted out everything without stopping to take a breath: "It was awesome! We beat the Ballymore Bears by a goal! Sammy and Chris dominated in the ruck, Mo marked everything that went into the backline, Mr Scott made some really cool moves, Joey came over and licked me at quarter-time, Jimmy and I both kicked three goals,

Hugo got 'falconed' again but I went over and told him not to worry about it, Jimmy's cousins ran all day, and at half-time we all got jelly snakes!"

After this bizarre match report, Fox had so many questions he didn't know where to start. After a short silence, he said, "Joey licked you at quarter-time?"

Fox couldn't wait to play with Chase in the following Saturday's game against the Romana Roosters.

Mace was in a foul mood in class on Monday. He was furious that the Diggers had managed to win all three games with six of their best players out of the team.

"Who cares, Swift?" said Mace while they were waiting for Mr Grinter to arrive. "We're going to pulverise you in the finals."

"Yeah we are so going to pulv ... pulvo ... pulvis ... pulvaris—whatever Mace just said," said Vince.

Mace was just about to tell Vince to shut up when Mr Renton suddenly walked into the classroom, sending the students scurrying to their seats.

The principal cleared his throat and said, "Mr Grinter has phoned to say he will be away for a few days."

"According to his message, he was attacked by a swarm of killer bees," he added, rolling his eyes.

Sally Renton went to write down this unbelievable

excuse, but then realised her dad was already there and put down her pen.

"A substitute teacher will be joining you after recess, and I trust you will give her your utmost attention."

Back in the classroom after recess, Fox asked Hugo, "Who do you think our substitute teacher will be?"

"Anyone would have to be better than Mr Grinter," said Hugo.

At that moment a blonde-haired woman wearing a colourful poncho and rose-tinted glasses entered the classroom. She had a white flower tucked behind her ear and was holding a guitar.

"Hey kids, my name's Rainbow Love," she said.

Rainbow Love was the twin sister of Miles Winter's personal assistant, Summer Love. Like her sister, Rainbow was a hippy and could be a little vague at times.

"Okay, so what was the last thing Mr Grinter was teaching you before he left?'

"He was talking about the Great Wall of China," said Chung.

"Cool," said Rainbow. "So construction on the Great wall of China first began around about AD220—"

Hugo's and Chung's hands shot up in the air.

"Yes?"

"It's more like 221BC, Miss," said Hugo.

"BC, AD—it doesn't really make much difference," said Rainbow.

"It makes more than 400 years difference!" said Chung.

Fox looked across at Sally, expecting her to be furiously scribbling down notes to pass on to her father. But instead she was sitting quietly with her hands clasped, smiling at Rainbow Love.

"I think there's a little song I need to sing you two. Would everyone like to hear a song?" said the new teacher.

"Yes, please," said Sally enthusiastically as Rainbow picked up her guitar.

"I call it *Chill Out*."

Rainbow then started to sing her original folk song.

If someone makes a little mistake
There's no need to scream or shout
Sit back, relax and take a breath
It's time to chill right out
If someone makes a statement
That is a teensy-weensy bit wrong
Instead of pointing out their flaws
Remember the words to this song.

Hugo and Chung looked at each other in disbelief. They could not comprehend a teacher saying it was fine to get the answers wrong!

Just chill out, you know you want to
Who cares who's wrong or right?

Let's all hold hands together
There's no need to yell or fight.

Rainbow finished the song by shutting her eyes and whispering,

"Shhhhhhhhhhh ... just chill out."

Hugo looked like he was about to be sick.

"I never thought I'd say this, but I actually miss Mr Grinter," he said to his friends at lunch.

Mr Renton decided to sit in on Rainbow Love's class to see how she was getting on, but when he walked into the classroom, he stopped and stared. His daughter was wearing a brightly coloured poncho and rose-tinted glasses with a flower behind her ear—just like her new teacher. "She wasn't wearing any of that at breakfast," he thought, frowning.

"Don't mind me," Mr Renton said as he moved to the back of the class.

"Cool," said Rainbow. "Okay kids, we're doing maths. Just say there are 100 people at a protest against global warming, and, like, 45 per cent of them get arrested unfairly by the police, how many protesters would remain?"

Three hands shot up in the air—Hugo's, Chung's and Sally's.

"Yes, Sally," said Rainbow.

"Um, 45?"

"Hey, way to go, girl—well done!" said the teacher.

"But that's wrong," said Hugo.

"It should be 55," said Chung.

"Tch-tch—I think it's time for another song," said Rainbow, picking up her guitar. "It's a song I wrote about maths, and it's called *Close Enough is Good Enough*."

The vein on the side of Mr Renton's temple started to pulse as Rainbow launched into another of her original songs:

Accuracy is overrated
Don't reward it with a prize
Who cares if your answer's right?
I'd rather look at a sunrise
Yes, close enough is good enough
Don't sweat it if you're wrong
If you're out by a tiny bit
Don't say sorry, just sing this song
Times tables aren't important
And fractions make me laugh
Would you rather be doing algebra
Or at the zoo with a giraffe?

The principal had heard enough. He left the classroom, pulled out his phone and dialled Mr Grinter's number.

"Blast—his answering machine!" said Mr Renton. "Um, Mr Grinter, it's Mr Renton. I hate leaving messages on these things. Anyway, I know you're supposedly recovering from a deadly attack by killer bees, but I need you back at work tomorrow. No excuses. If you aren't here, don't bother coming back—ever!"

Mr Renton would normally have felt bad about leaving a message like that, but he knew Mr Grinter was faking his illness and didn't want that hippy Rainbow Love teaching his daughter for another minute!

The next morning, a very sheepish Mr Renton walked into the classroom. "Good news, students," he said. "Mr Grinter is back!"

Sally scowled, while Hugo and Chung high-fived each other.

But when Mr Grinter walked into the room, the students stared at him in horror.

Their teacher looked like a character from a zombie film. His face was completely swollen and he had red marks all over his face, neck and arms.

"Oh my God!" said Lewis. "I think his story about the bees might have actually been true!"

The Diggers' next match was a special one for Fox, as it was the first time he and Chase would play on the same team.

"Don't feel like you have to pass to me all the time," said Chase.

"Okay then," said Fox with a grin.

"But don't ignore me if I'm in a good position!" said Chase in alarm.

As usual, Fox and his family were early. He and Chase entered the Roosters' changing rooms together, said hi to Mr Scott, and picked up a *Record* from the table.

Fox turned to the 'On This Day' page and read about Mr Scott's exploits from four decades ago:

> On this day 40 years ago ... the Davinal Diggers enjoyed a resounding victory over the Shepton Sharks, with Diggers sharpshooter Greg Scott kicking 14 goals. The Sharks had two taggers on Scott throughout the day, but they could not curtail the champion's brilliance. Greg Scott is well on his way to winning another League Best and Fairest Award ...

In his record, Chase was looking at the results from the previous round:

Davinal Diggers 10.6 (66) d Ballymore Bears 8.12 (60)
Best: R. Officer (B.O.G.), C. Wek, S. Saaed, C. Swift, J. Rioli.
Goals: C. Swift 3, J. Rioli 3, C. Wek 2, S. Saaed 2.

"What are you smiling at?" asked Fox.

"Nothing," said Chase—but in truth he was absolutely thrilled that Mr Scott had included him and Jimmy in the best players.

Chase also studied the ladder and was very pleased to see that the Diggers were currently sitting second. He was not so pleased to see that the Dragons were on top with an incredible percentage.

	P	W	L	Pts	%
Davinal Dragons	5	5	0	20	433.67
Davinal Diggers	5	4	1	16	123.03
Shepton Sharks	5	4	1	16	115.77
Stonewarren Stingrays	5	3	2	12	160.53
Colbran Cockatoos	5	3	2	12	122.73
Romana Roosters	5	3	2	12	107.79
Tennant Hill Tigers	5	3	2	12	104.89
Ballymore Bears	5	2	3	8	80.26
Linmore Leopards	5	2	3	8	53.66
Gregtown Goannas	5	1	4	4	89.68
Firbush Fever	5	0	5	0	31.19
Morgan Bridge Magpies	5	0	5	0	23.06

After the teams ran out on to the ground, Fox went over and flipped the coin with Ed Gillies, the friendly captain of the Roosters. Appropriately, Ed's hair stood straight up in the middle, just like a rooster's crest.

"Hey Fox," he said while they waited for the umpire to toss the coin, "I saw on the team sheet there were two Swifts—don't tell me there's another one just like you?!"

"That's my younger brother, Chase. He's not like me—he's much better!"

"Oh. My. God," thought Ed. And for the first time in his life, his smile deserted him.

Just before the start of the game, Fox stood in the middle of the oval with Sammy, Rosie and Chung. After a quick chat about their tactics for the first bounce, Fox looked downfield into the Diggers' forward line.

"Wow," he thought as he watched Simon, Chris, Paige, Chase and Jimmy take up their positions. "I would hate to be a backman playing against a forward line with those guys in it."

As soon as the ball was bounced, Sammy tapped the ball to Fox, who handballed it to Rosie as she flashed past. Rosie kicked a beautiful pass to Paige, who marked the ball out in front of her eyes and played on immediately. She drew a player and handballed over the top to Chase, who quickly handballed to Jimmy, who pinpointed a pass on to the chest of Simon in the goalsquare.

"I got dizzy watching that!" yelled out Lewis.

Fox kicked three goals in the first quarter, but his

favourite moment came when he picked up the ball on the half-forward flank and spotted Chase making a lead in the pocket. He drilled a low pass, which Chase dived for and caught like a slips catch in cricket, just centimetres off the ground. The crowd cheered and the spectators in cars honked their horns to show their appreciation.

Fox watched his brother settle himself, then kick a perfect drop punt through the goals from a very tight angle.

"Not bad, little bro," said Fox, high-fiving Chase.

"Next time make the pass a bit harder—that was too easy!" said Chase, with a cheeky grin.

Back in the middle Ed Gillies shook his head and said to Fox, "Please tell me you don't have any more brothers or sisters!"

By quarter-time the game was nearly all over.

Roosters: 1.1 (7)
Visitors: 13.4 (82)

But as he had done all season, Mr Scott started taking off the star Diggers players in order to give everyone a fair go. This meant the game became a bit more of an even contest from then on.

As much as Fox hated being off the ground for a second—let alone a whole quarter—it was good to watch some of the less skilled players improving because they were being given decent **match time**. And when the team won, everyone felt part of it because everyone had played three of the four quarters.

At one point during the game, Fox looked over at Mr Scott and standing next to him was a supporter he hadn't seen at a Diggers game before—Samantha Lu!

"You sly dog, Mr Scott!" thought Fox.

Lewis was talking to Samantha and she could not stop laughing.

"So Miss Lu, if you're taking out my coach tonight, I want him back home no later than 10pm, okay?" said Lewis.

"Okay," said Samantha with a smile.

"Oh, and don't think I'm letting you two go out on a date on your own!"

"So are you coming with us?"

"I'm not—but she is!" said Lewis, pointing to Joey.

The game finished with the Diggers winning comfortably by 68 points.

Roosters:	9.9 (63)
Visitors:	20.11 (131)

Fox discovered that the best thing about playing footy with your brother was you could keep talking about the game for hours when you got home.

Mrs Swift didn't agree that this was a good thing at all, and that night at dinner she put her foot down.

"Boys, I am sick of all this footy talk! From now on you can only talk about football if it comes up naturally in the conversation. Okay?"

Fox and Chase rolled their eyes and moaned, "All right, Mum."

"Chase, can you please pass the salt?" said Mr Swift.

"Did you say *pass* the salt, Dad? Well, speaking of passes, what about that *pass* Fox kicked to me in the pocket?!"

"Yeah, the way you marked that *pass* was so cool, Chase," said Fox with a grin.

Mrs Swift looked at her husband, smiled and rolled her eyes. "I give up!" she sighed.

The season progressed well for the Diggers, although there were some pretty weird experiences along the way.

When the team arrived for the game against the Morgan Bridge Magpies, Fox was surprised to see a flock of sheep on the oval.

The coach of the Magpies explained that the club couldn't afford a mower, so they used sheep to trim the grass instead by letting them graze on the field.

Fox thought this was a really cool idea—until the flock was herded away to reveal the playing area was covered in sheep droppings. Needless to say, no one from either side dived on the ground to win the ball that day. No one, that is, except for Mo, who said, "Bitsashepooneerhutnawun!"

Paige translated this to mean, "A bit of sheep poo never hurt anyone!"

"It's a good thing they don't use cows," said Lewis. "Can you imagine having to play in the mess caused by a herd of lawn-mooers?"

Despite the "slippery" conditions, the Diggers managed to win by a whopping 88 points.

In the game against the Colbran Cockatoos, the players received a nasty shock when they discovered a snake curled up in the centre circle. The umpire went over to explain to the parents that it was only a harmless tree snake, but Hugo told all the players it was a lethal tiger snake. Both teams were terrified, and whenever the ball landed near the snake during the match, Hugo was the only one game enough to go and pick it up. As a result, Hugo easily had the most possessions of any game in his career, and even managed to be named in the best players for the first time.

Unfortunately, Hugo's form in the other games was not as good as he would have liked. In the game against the Gregtown Goannas, he got hit by a rare "double falcon" when the ball bounced off his head into the goalpost, then off the goalpost and back on to his head.

On the plus side, Hugo's relationship with Bruno was improving. Against the Linmore Leopards, Bruno had stepped in to help Hugo after a Leopards player called 'Sniper' White pushed him over.

"You got a problem with Hugo, then you got a problem with me!" Bruno warned. Sniper kept well clear of Hugo for the rest of the game.

Much to Hugo's delight, he also noticed that Bruno would often try to kick the ball to him, even when he wasn't the best option.

As captain, Fox could not have been happier with the Diggers' performances. They were winning every week—not by anywhere near as much as the Dragons were, but they were still winning, and had bonded as a team. And what Fox enjoyed the most about winning was when the team formed a circle in the changing rooms and sang the Diggers club song.

At the start of the season Mr Scott had announced it was time for the Diggers to let go of the past and look to the future.

"I love our old club song and it holds many wonderful memories for me," he had said, "but this is an exciting new era for the club and a time for new beginnings. That's why, over the break, I came up with a new club song."

This was a big change and the players went silent. Everyone prayed it wouldn't be really lame. But when

Mr Scott told them what the song would be and put the words up on the whiteboard, they smiled. A few wins later, the players had learned all the words and now they absolutely loved singing it.

It went like this:

Oh we're from Diggerland
A fighting fury, we're from Diggerland
In any weather you will see us with a grin
Risking head and shin
If we're behind, then never mind we'll fight and
fight and win
For we're from Diggerland
We never weaken 'til the final siren's gone
Like the Diggers of old
We're strong and we're bold
Oh we're from Digger ...

YELLOW AND BLUE!
For we're from Diggerland!

Fox especially liked how everyone yelled out:

YELLOW AND BLUE!

"Do you think we can beat the Dragons if we play them in the finals?" asked Chase after they had sung the song one day.

"It would take a miracle—but miracles do happen," said Fox, remembering Hugo's grubber goal in last year's Grand Final.

14

This Means Wardrobe

After a brilliant 83-point win against the Linmore Leopards in the final round, the Diggers seemed in good shape for the finals.

Fox turned to the sports section of the *Davinal Digest* and carefully studied the ladder.

	P	W	L	Pts	%
Davinal Dragons	11	11	0	44	368.56
Davinal Diggers	11	10	1	40	158.94
Shepton Sharks	11	8	3	32	128.26
Stonewarren Stingrays	11	8	3	32	115.03
Colbran Cockatoos	11	6	5	24	101.32
Tennant Hill Tigers	11	5	6	20	97.23

Romana Roosters	11	5	6	20	96.95
Ballymore Bears	11	5	6	20	81.62
Gregtown Goannas	11	4	7	16	112.59
Linmore Leopards	11	3	8	12	57.02
Morgan Bridge Magpies	11	1	10	4	27.82
Firbush Fever	11	0	11	0	33.91

"I think we can beat the Dragons," he said to himself.

"I think the Diggers can beat us," said Miles Winter, slapping the sports section of the newspaper on the kitchen table.

"No way, Dad," said Mace. "They still have some complete battlers in their team."

"Yeah, like 'Falcon' Trippitt!" said Vince, who had slept over at the Winters' house.

"Even so, it would be nice if we had some *insurance*— if you know what I mean," said Miles.

Mace grinned and said, "I know exactly what you mean, Dad."

"Yeah, nice one, Mr Winter ... By the way, um ... what's 'insurance'?" said Vince.

Miles looked at Vince in disbelief for a second before turning to his son and saying, "I'll leave it with you to come up with something, Mace. Don't let me down."

Not surprisingly, it took Mace only 10 minutes to come up with an incredibly evil plan.

"We're going to 'egg' the principal's house!" he told Vince triumphantly.

"But won't we get into trouble?" asked Vince.

"The principal won't know it's us, you idiot," said Mace. "After we've thrown the eggs, we'll leave some fake egging plans at the scene, and they'll have the names of Swift and his mates all over them!"

"But won't that get Swift and his mates into trouble?" said Vince, who was once again pretty slow on the uptake.

"That's the whole point!" yelled Mace. "They'll have Saturday detentions for all of the finals and most of next year!"

Mace took all the eggs out of the fridge, and borrowed his younger twin brothers' textas to draw up the fake plans. He put these items into a backpack and nodded at Vince.

"Time to go?" asked Vince.

"Eggs-actly," said Mace.

But Vince didn't laugh.

"Don't you get it?" said Mace. "*Eggs*-actly, because we're throwing eggs—it's a clever play on words."

"Yeah, I get it," said Vince.

"Well, *you* do one then!" snapped Mace.

"Okay, um, how about ... let's *milk* this for all it's worth."

"Milk? We're not throwing *milk* at Mr Renton's house, you idiot! I don't know why I bother. Come on, let's go."

On the way, Mace and Vince had to ride past Chung's house. As they got closer, they saw that the roller door to the Lees' garage was up, and standing inside the garage were Fox, Rosie, Lewis and Chung.

Mace's heart skipped a beat. He and Vince jumped off their bikes and dived into a nearby bush to spy on their enemies.

They watched as all four Diggers stepped into a giant wardrobe at the back of the garage.

"This is too good to be true!" whispered Mace.

As soon as Fox and his friends were inside the wardrobe, Mace ran up and turned the key in the lock. He figured that if they were all locked up while the egging took place, none of them would have an alibi that could be backed up by an adult.

"Not that he'll even know about the egging until it's too late," thought Mace with a smile. "He won't even know who locked him in the closet!"

But Mace had forgotten he was with Vince.

"Hey, you Diggers losers!" yelled Vince at the closet door. "You guys are going to have so much *egg* on your faces—just like the principal's house!"

"Shut up, Vince!" roared Mace.

"But 'egg on your faces' was a really clever play on words—"

Mace and Vince bolted out of the garage, hopped back on their bikes and rode off towards their egging target.

What the two bullies didn't realise was that it wasn't just any old wardrobe they had locked the Diggers in. This was a special piece of furniture handcrafted by Mo and Snowy Davison for Chung to use in his magic act, and at the back they had built in a secret exit.

Chung slid back a panel and pushed a button and he and his friends jumped out of the closet into the fresh air.

"What was that all about?" said Rosie.

"I thought I heard Vince talking about egging the principal's house," said Chung.

"Uh-oh!" said Fox.

"What's the matter?" asked Lewis.

"They're going to frame us again!" cried Fox. "We have to stop them!"

Mr Renton's house was about 5 kilometres away, but the Diggers had no choice but to start running.

Meanwhile, Mace and Vince had been held up at the train tracks.

"No way!" said Mace. "Only two trains go through Davinal each day and we get held up by one of them!"

As soon as the train had passed, the boys started pedalling furiously and didn't stop until they arrived at Mr Renton's house. After checking to make sure no one was around, Mace quickly stripped off his backpack and took out all the eggs and the fake egging plans.

He hurled the first egg, which went "splat" as it hit the front door, then Vince made a direct hit on a window on the second floor. They had managed to throw another three eggs each by the time Fox and his friends appeared at the end of the street.

"It's Swift!" yelled Mace. "Let's go!"

Mace dumped the egging plans on the ground, picked up his backpack and was about to make a getaway when a police car came out of nowhere and pulled up in front of them.

The local policeman, Lex Hunt, was dropping Mr Renton back home after the two of them had had lunch together.

When Mace and Vince saw the police car, they froze. Fox and his friends quickly hid behind some bushes before they could be spotted.

"Oi! What are you two doing?!" said Sergeant Hunt, jumping out of his car.

Sergeant Hunt was a tall man with a large stomach, and he made Mace very nervous.

"Um, well, we were just riding by when we saw a kid called, err, Fox Swift and a few of his mates throwing eggs at the principal's house. So we ran over to, you know, stop them and they dropped their egging plans on the ground here, and ran off."

Sergeant Hunt looked at Mace doubtfully. He picked up the plans from the ground, studied them, and then slowly turned his gaze to Vince.

"Is this true, young man?" he asked in a booming voice.

Mace held his breath.

"It sure is. I definitely saw Fox Swift and his mates," said Vince confidently, and Mace breathed out with relief.

But then Vince added, "They must have somehow escaped out of the wardrobe we locked them in."

"Shut up, Vince!" said Mace out of the corner of his mouth.

"What?! Take us to this wardrobe *now*!" ordered Sergeant Hunt.

"Okay, let's hurry!" said Mace, pointing to the police car.

"There is no way Swift and his stupid mates will be able to get back to Chung's in time," Mace thought smugly. "And if they aren't in the wardrobe when we get there, Sergeant Hunt and Mr Renton will have to believe Vince and I are telling the truth."

Fox, Rosie, Lewis and Chung watched the police car drive off and began running. Fox knew they had little chance of getting to Chung's place before Sergeant Hunt, but they had to try.

Mace gave Sergeant Hunt Chung's address then said, "Shouldn't you turn on the siren and hurry up?"

"It's only five minutes away—there's no need for sirens," said the policeman in a gruff voice.

They were just approaching the train tracks when the lights started flashing and the boom gates went down.

"You have got to be kidding me!" cried Mace in frustration. "Stopped by two trains in one day—what are the odds?!"

"Mmm, let's see," said Vince. "There are two trains and 24 hours in a day, so if each train takes, say, five minutes to go by, that would be ... mmm, carry the five, multiply by three ..."

Mace watched as Vince put on a thoughtful expression while trying to calculate the odds.

"It's a one in 178.27 chance," said Vince.

"You just made that up, didn't you?"

"Um ... yes," said Vince.

Mace was about to yell, but let it go because the train was gone and they were on the move again.

"Excellent!" thought Mace. "We'll still get there ages before those losers!"

Mace turned to high-five Vince, but the car braked sharply and their hands missed.

"What are we stopping for?" asked Mace.

"There's a little white rabbit on the road," said the sergeant. He honked the horn, but the rabbit didn't move.

"Hey, cool—it's Gary!" said Vince.

"It's *not cool*," snapped Mace before inching forward to talk to Sergeant Hunt. "Why don't you just run over it?"

"What? I'm not going to deliberately run over a rabbit!" said the sergeant, taking off his seat belt.

He got out of the car and started talking to Gary. "Come on, little fella—off you go, off you go now," he said in a baby voice.

Mace could not believe it. "He should be shooting that pesky rabbit, not talking to it!" he thought. "What's the point of having a gun if he's not going to use it?"

Eventually Gary hopped away, but Mace was furious at the amount of time it had cost them.

The police car drove on, but was soon confronted by yet another obstacle. This time it was a kangaroo standing in the middle of the road.

"It's Joey!" said Vince.

"Make it roadkill!" yelled Mace.

"What did you say?!" cried Sergeant Hunt as he once again slammed on the brakes.

"I said, um, 'Look, a roo, um, standing still,'" said Mace unconvincingly.

"Just relax, Mace—this is what living in the country is all about," said Sergeant Hunt as he slowly got out of the car.

"Shoo, shoo," he said to Joey.

Mace rolled his eyes and thought, "Surely he could at least use his taser!"

While everyone was distracted by the kangaroo, Fox and his friends sprinted along a ridge above the road.

"Joey, you are a legend," thought Fox.

But even though they were now ahead of the police car, he knew they would soon be overtaken. That was when Lewis spotted a detour sign lying by the side of the road.

"Wait up, guys!" he said. "I've got an idea."

Mace was fuming in the back of the police car. First

a train, then a rabbit and then a kangaroo! But at least they were on their way again—and even though the Diggers were all fantastic runners, there was no way they could beat a car. They were only two minutes from Chung's place now. Mace put his hands behind his head and started to relax.

"Uh-oh," said Sergeant Hunt. "Looks like we're going to have to make a detour."

"What?!" cried Mace.

"Stephens Street is closed off," said Sergeant Hunt, pointing to a detour sign in the middle of the road. "We'll have to go the long way around. It'll only take us an extra 10 minutes."

"Noooooooooooooooooooooooooo!" thought Mace.

The Diggers raced into the Lees' garage just as the police car turned into the street. Chung opened the secret panel at the back of the wardrobe and they all jumped inside. Less than a minute later they heard the key being turned in the lock.

Fox, Lewis, Chung and Rosie fell out of the wardrobe, puffing and panting as if they had nearly run out of air. It was a very convincing performance given that, apart from Rosie, they were all exhausted from their frantic run.

Sergeant Hunt gave Mace and Vince a withering look.

"You could have killed them!" he bellowed. "And how could these four have possibly thrown eggs at the principal's house if they were locked in this wardrobe the whole time?"

"Don't worry, Lex," said Mr Renton, "I will be giving these two boys the most severe punishment possible."

"Looks like it's Saturday detentions for Mace and Vince," thought Fox. "That means they won't be able to play in the finals!"

"Sunday detentions?!"

Paige was furious. She had been ever since Mace and Vince had walked into class on Monday morning boasting about the punishment Mr Renton had given them.

"How come *we* got Saturday detentions and missed football games, and you and Vince get Sunday detentions so you can still play?"

"Who cares?" snapped Mace. "There's nothing you can do about it!"

"Yes, there is!" said Hugo. "We're going to see the principal."

At lunchtime Fox, Hugo, Paige, Lewis, Rosie and Chung made their way to the principal's office.

When they got there Miss Carey was nowhere in sight, but Fox could almost sense her presence. Suddenly he looked up and saw her hanging from the light fitting. She was cleaning it with a cotton tip.

"What do you want?" she barked, looking down at them.

"We need to see Mr Renton straight away!" said Hugo.

"Well, Mr Renton is doing some very important work at the moment and cannot possibly be disturbed—"

At that moment Mr Renton burst out of his office. "Miss Carey, I just checked my footy tipping," he said, wiggling his hips in a weird sort of dance. "I tipped nine winners—yessssssssssssss! Oh—"

As soon as the principal realised he had visitors, he stopped his victory dance, stood up straight and cleared his throat.

"Um, what's going on?" he asked.

"Mr Renton, we'd like to talk to you about something," said Fox.

"Okay, but you'll have to make it quick because I'm pretty busy," said Mr Renton.

"We promise we won't keep you from your footy tipping for long," said Paige.

"Well, what is it?" Mr Renton asked when they were all in his office.

"How come you gave Mace and Vince Sunday detentions and not Saturday detentions?" asked Hugo.

"Well, Sunday detentions are even more serious than Saturday detentions," said Mr Renton.

"Really?" Chung said doubtfully. "I didn't know that."

"I didn't know that either," admitted Mr Renton, "but Mr Winter assured me that—"

"Mr Winter?! Well that explains everything," said Paige.

Mr Renton suddenly realised that Miles had tricked him—but he didn't want the students to know.

"Anyway, why am I explaining myself to you? Some of you are the thieves who stole my apples! Now get back to class immediately."

As the disappointed Diggers stood up to leave, Hugo noticed the master key hanging on the wall.

"Mr Renton, does that master key open all the lockers?"

"Yes, it does."

Hugo then started pacing back and forth with his arms clasped behind his back.

"And on the day your apples disappeared, was Mr Winter at the school?" he asked.

"As a matter of fact, he was," said Mr Renton. "He borrowed some books on hip-hop dancing and dressmaking."

A horrible image suddenly appeared in Lewis' mind. "And during this visit was there any time when your attention was distracted?" asked Hugo.

"Well, I suppose when I was getting the books down," said Mr Renton. "They were both on the top shelf, you see."

HIP HOP FLOP

"Just one final question, Mr Renton," said Hugo. "Did Mr Winter leave the room while he was with you?"

"Mmmm, yes he did—a couple of times," said Mr Renton, recalling the trips Miles took to the toilet.

"I thought so!" cried Hugo triumphantly. "Mr Renton, I put it to you that Mr Winter took the master key, slipped it to Mace through a window and framed the Diggers players."

"Oh, come on," said Mr Renton. "I mean, even Miles isn't that evil."

But the more he thought about it, the more it made sense. He had never heard Miles talk about dressmaking or hip-hop dancing before—or since—that day. And it had been Miles who had brought up the locker search. And Miles had been the one to suggest giving the culprits Saturday detentions.

"Okay, maybe he *is* that evil," said Mr Renton. "But unfortunately there's nothing I can do about it now."

"Yes, there is," said Hugo. "You can remove all references to the stolen apples from their school records."

"Well, I suppose I could do that," said the principal. "Miss Carey, come in here, please!"

Miss Carey poked her head inside the office so quickly that Fox guessed she must have been listening at the door.

"I want you to destroy all the student records relating to the apple thefts straight away."

Miss Carey gave a deep sigh and returned to her desk. As the Diggers left, they noticed she was cutting up the offending records with the tiniest pair of nail scissors they had ever seen.

"I admire her attention to detail," whispered Lewis, "but that's going to take her *at least* three days!"

During the week leading up to the finals, Miles Winter received an email from Jacko's dad.

Dear Miles,

I am writing to you on behalf of all the parents
of the Dragons recruits. We wish to inform you
that if you want our boys to play in the finals, you
will need to pay us a 'Finals Bonus' of $100 per
player. There should also be a bonus incentive
scheme where players are paid $20 for each goal
they kick and an extra $100 if they are named in
the best players.

If you refuse this request, then all the boys will
come down with the flu and will not be able to play.

Have a nice day,

Mark Jackson

Miles sat back and considered the email. He decided
that paying the players for kicking goals and being in
the best players could actually make them even hungrier
to succeed.

"And anyway," he thought, "there's plenty of money
in the Tilley Fawcett Inheritance Trust Account!"

So he simply replied:

Done.

15

A Final Bonus

The fixture for the first week of the finals was all set:

Davinal Dragons v Davinal Diggers
Shepton Sharks v Stonewarren Stingrays

At training on the Thursday night before the first final, Fox explained to Chase how the system worked.

"It's really quite simple," he said. "The winner of the Dragons-Diggers clash goes straight into the Grand Final so they have a week off the next week, while the loser is playing the winner of the Sharks-Stingrays game. Whoever loses the game in the second week is out, but the winner of that game goes into the Grand Final to play the team that won the first game."

"Say what?" said Chase.

"The most important thing to remember is that we finished in the top two, so we get the double chance," said Fox.

"So ... even if we lose to the Dragons in the first game, we are still alive?"

"Yep," said Fox before quickly adding, "not that we're going to lose!"

Mr Scott stood in the middle of the ground and called for the Diggers to run over. Players sprinted in from all directions and huddled in front of him.

"Cyril Rioli has sent through a really cool training drill to get us focused and firing for the finals," said Mr Scott. "A few of you have been having your kicks **smothered** lately so we are going to practise how to baulk and sidestep your opponent to avoid this."

The Diggers listened eagerly as Mr Scott explained the drill.

"We're going to break up into three groups: Group A next to the giant cucumber; Group B next to the enormous bunch of carrots; and Group C next to the massive watermelon. A player from Group A will run with the footy as a player from Group B comes out to tackle them. At the same time, someone from Group C will call for the player from Group A to kick the ball to them."

Mr Scott held up a diagram to make his instructions clearer. Fox liked the way his coach used drawings with his explanations, because some of the kids seemed to understand a lot better when they could picture the drills.

THE BAULK/SIDESTEP DRILL

What you need:

1. A football
2. Divide team equally into two (25m apart – A&C), with 2 players positioned about 10m away—see B & D—to act as the smotherers

To run the drill:

A runs at **B**

A motions to kick; **B** attempts to smother

A avoids the smother by stopping the kicking action and sidestepping **B**

Once **A** is past **B**, the player should straighten, steady and kick to **C**

The drill repeats with **C** mirroring the movements of **A** and with **D** acting as the smotherer

Rotate kickers and smotherers so each player attempts the smother.

"Okay, just as the player from Group A goes to kick the ball, the player from Group B will try to smother it. But just before the player goes to kick the ball, they stop, sidestep the would-be 'smotherer', steady themselves and pass the ball accurately to the player from Group C. Is that clear?"

Most of the players nodded but a few had confused looks on their faces.

"Before we start the drill, I'll do a quick demonstration with Fox and Chase," said Mr Scott.

This was the other thing Fox loved—whenever their coach introduced a new training drill, he actually showed the kids how to do it properly.

Mr Scott handballed a footy to Fox and told Chase to stand about 40 metres away.

"So, Fox is in Group A, I'm in Group B and Chase is in Group C," he said.

Fox ran towards his coach and made as if he were going to kick the footy to Chase. Mr Scott went to smother the kick, but at the last second Fox pulled the ball back in towards his stomach, sidestepped around the coach to the left and speared a perfect pass to Chase, who had led out towards him.

"Well done to the Swift boys!" called out Mr Scott. "And if you guys want to do some 'homework', just go to YouTube and check out some clips of Cyril Rioli—he is the best at baulking and sidestepping I have ever seen."

Fox wished the teachers at school would set homework like that.

Mr Scott added that Cyril had given him a few important tips on how to sidestep players.

"Make sure you cut hard when you change direction, and use your eyes to make your opponent think you are going one way, when really you are going to go the other," he told them.

There was a terrific atmosphere at training that night, with everyone encouraging each other and having fun. Fox was sure the Diggers would play well against the Dragons on Saturday.

The Dragons had finished on top of the ladder, so the game was at their home ground. Despite it being an away game for the Diggers, lots of their fans turned up to cheer them on. Fox noticed that his club had fans of all ages—Matilda Wall, who had brought along Gary the rabbit, was there, chatting to the 88-year-old Snowy Davison, and so were a number of much younger supporters, like Amanda Trippitt, who was wearing a Diggers jumper with Bruno's No. 22 on the back.

You could have heard a pin drop while Mr Scott was addressing his team in the changing rooms before the start of the game. He didn't rant, rave or yell, but his message was clear: "Go out there, run, chase, tackle and support each other. I want to hear lots of talk and lots of encouragement. As long as you give 100 per cent in every contest all day, you can walk off the ground feeling proud. Is that what you're going to do?"

"Yesssssssssss!" cried all the Diggers players.

The speech by the coach of the Dragons was not so positive.

"Any player who makes a mistake will be **dragged** immediately!" yelled Miles.

He was so loud that Fox and his teammates could hear him through the wall.

"Hmm," said Lewis, "he sounds like a Dalek from *Doctor Who*!" This made the Diggers players crack up, and their coach laughed so hard he had to sit down.

Hearing the laughter next door, Mr Winter lowered his voice.

"Here's how we're going to win," he said. "Don't kick the ball anywhere near the good Diggers players."

"Huh?" said Vince

"I'll spell it out for you: don't kick the ball near any of the following players—"

Mr Winter turned to the whiteboard next to him and read out the list of names written on it.

"Fox Swift, Chris, Sammy, Mo Officer, Paige, Bruno, Simon Phillips, Chung, the girl with the ponytail—"

"That's Rosie," said Vince enthusiastically, causing Mace to glare at him.

"Whatever," said Mr Winter, continuing with his list, "… Chase Swift and Lewis Rioli."

"But that's 11 players," pointed out Vince.

"Fortunately Greg Scott is a stupid coach who often has a lot of these guys sitting on the bench, which makes your job much easier," said Mr Winter. He then pointed to the list of names.

"So what will happen if any of you kick the ball near these guys?"

"We get dragged," came the unenthusiastic response from the Dragons.

After Joey and Gary led the Diggers out on to the field, Fox jogged over to the centre of the ground for the toss of the coin.

The umpire was a very short man, and Fox instantly recognised him as Mr Bigg, the owner of Bigg Print, who had designed the invitation to the Diggers' Night of Talent.

"Hey Fox," he said in a friendly voice. Mace, who was also there for the toss, rolled his eyes.

"It's the away captain's call, so what do you want, Fox—heads or tails?"

"Tails," said Fox.

After inspecting the coin closely, the umpire said, "It's heads."

Fox could not believe it. Hugo had assured him he had an equal chance of winning the toss each time, yet he had only won twice in all the games he'd played this season.

"Woohoo! We'll kick that way," said Mace, pointing to the end where a small wind was blowing.

"Okay, shake hands, you two," said Mr Bigg.

Fox extended his hand but Mace, as usual, refused to shake it.

Mr Bigg was very unimpressed by this. There was nothing he hated more than bad sportsmanship.

"Mace, if you don't shake hands right now, I'll send you off and you can sit on the bench for the first 15 minutes of the match."

"You can't do that," said Mace defiantly.

"I can and I will."

Mr Bigg then called Miles over.

"Coach, your captain has refused to shake hands with the Diggers captain, so he will not be allowed on the field until 15 minutes into the first quarter."

"That's the stupidest decision I have ever heard," said Miles. "Do you have any idea who I am?"

"Yes, you're the coach who is about to cost his team a free kick," replied Mr Bigg.

"You'd better not do that," warned Miles.

"Is that a threat?" asked the umpire.

"You bet it is!" roared Miles.

"Your free kick, Fox," said Mr Bigg calmly.

"But the game hasn't even started yet, you idiot!" screamed Miles.

"That's a 25-metre penalty."

Miles continued his tirade. "You can't give free kicks and 25-metre penalties before the game has even started, you fool!"

In response, Mr Bigg simply blew his whistle and said, "That's another 25!"

With Miles still screeching abuse at the umpire, Fox casually booted the ball through the goals from less than a metre out. The Diggers were six points in front before the players had even taken up their positions.

Miles appeared to be frothing at the mouth, and had to be dragged off the ground by several parents of the Dragons players.

"Miles, if you cost the Dragons one more goal, don't expect the boys to play in the Grand Final—and I don't care how much money you pay us!" said an unimpressed Mr Jackson.

It was right at this moment that the kookaburra that lived at the Dragons' ground started laughing.

"That stupid bird!" screamed Miles. "I am going to—"

Miles looked around and spotted the wildlife officer, Bill Kelso, standing behind him with his arms folded and a stern look on his face.

"... uh, find some worms and feed it a nice dinner," he said quickly.

Mr Jackson handed Miles a brown paper bag and said, "Breathe into this and get a hold of yourself!"

Breathing into the paper bag didn't help, but Miles was eventually calmed down by the way the Dragons performed in the first quarter. With Mo Officer sitting on the bench, the Dragons full-forward, Sandy Barr, was unstoppable and kicked four goals. The Dragons players were very disciplined, always trying to kick the ball to a teammate who wasn't playing on one of the Diggers' stars.

To make matters worse, as soon as Mace was allowed on to the ground, he managed to kick a goal. Afterwards, he ran around and skidded along the ground on his knees, the way international soccer players do after they score.

"Good to see it's not all about you, Mace!" called out Lewis. The supporters nearby burst out laughing and Mace went bright red.

Fox was playing brilliantly, taking some spectacular marks and kicking several amazing goals, but the Diggers trailed by more than four goals at quarter-time.

| Dragons | 8.3 (51) |
| Visitors | 4.2 (26) |

On the way to their quarter-time huddles, Mace jogged past Fox and said, "It's only going to get worse, loser!"

Unfortunately, this was one of the rare occasions when Mace was right.

With Bruno sitting on the bench in the second quarter, the Dragons' centre half-forward, Jacko, started to dominate. He took 10 marks for the quarter and kicked five goals straight. To make matters worse, Hugo went for a mark on the wing and copped another falcon.

By half-time the Dragons' lead had blown out to 44 points.

| Dragons | 14.6 (90) |
| Visitors | 7.4 (46) |

The Diggers were more competitive in the second half. This was mainly because their two key defenders were back on the ground, which prevented Sandy and Jacko from kicking easy goals.

There were also some individual highlights for the

Diggers that gave their supporters something to cheer about. Mo Officer burst through a pack in the back pocket and emerged with the ball, leaving four dazed Dragon forwards lying stunned on the ground. Chase goaled with a sensational **bicycle kick** over his head, and Jimmy kicked a magnificent grubber goal on his **wrong foot** from the boundary line.

But with Fox, Paige, Sammy, Chung and Rosie all spending a quarter on the bench, it was very difficult to make any inroads into the Dragons' lead.

The final scoreboard read:

Dragons	18.10 (118)
Visitors	11.7 (73)

The Dragons had won by 45 points.

Fox hated losing to the Dragons, but he knew that the Diggers players had all tried as hard as they could. The Dragons were also an incredibly talented team with stars in every single position—it was no disgrace to be beaten by a quality opponent.

As Fox went around shaking hands with his opponents, he noticed there seemed to be a lack of team spirit among the Dragons players. Apart from Mace and Vince, none of them seemed very happy to win.

During the game, he recalled, even when a Dragons player kicked a goal, there was little enthusiasm shown by his teammates.

"It's a bit like playing against robots," he thought to himself.

Lewis came over and patted him on the back. "Hey Foxy, mun," he said in a West Indian accent, "you'll get 'em next time."

"Yep, we will," said Fox, though deep down he knew it was very unlikely. They would also have to beat either the Stingrays or the Sharks next week just to get the chance to try.

As Hugo was leaving the field, he walked past Jacko, who was chatting to his father.

"Well done, son," Mr Jackson was saying. "Five goals—at $20 a goal, that's a $100 bonus!"

"Mmm," thought Hugo, "that information might come in handy if we play them again in the Grand Final."

School on the Monday was unbearable for the Diggers players. Mace and Vince took any opportunity they could to rub in the Dragons' victory.

Fortunately, Vince wasn't very good at helping Mace deliver his nasty taunts.

"Knock, knock!" said Mace in a loud voice near where Fox and Lewis were sitting.

"What?" said Vince, looking confused.

"You're supposed to say, 'Who's there?'!"

"Oh yeah, sorry, Mace. Umm ... who's there?"

"Diggersar."

"Who's there?"

"Vince, you idiot—you're supposed to say, 'Diggersar who?'!"

"But you just said to say, 'Who's there?'"

"And now I want you say 'Diggersar who?'!"

"Oh, I get it—this is one of those knock-knock jokes!"

"Yes! So ... knock, knock!"

"Who's there?"

"Diggersar."

"Diggersar who?"

But before Mace could answer, Lewis jumped in and said, "Diggers are a team that don't pay their players—unlike the cheating Dragons."

Fox gave Lewis a high five.

"Mace! Why would you tell a knock-knock joke like that?" asked a stunned Vince.

"That wasn't the joke, you idiot—Lewis changed the ending."

Fox cracked up laughing.

"Laugh it up, Swift," said Mace. "The Stingrays will probably thrash you this week, but I actually hope you win—so we can absolutely humiliate you in the Grand Final."

"Yeah, we are so going to fumigate you!" said Vince. He had obviously misheard what Mace had said.

Fox always liked playing against the Stonewarren Stingrays. They had a really cool captain called Rob 'The Birdman' Stewart. He was called 'The Birdman' because he often soared into the air to take spectacular marks. The dreadlocks in his hair made his marking even more eye-catching.

In a game between the two teams earlier in the year, the Birdman and Fox had put on an incredible display of high marking, both pulling down screamer after screamer all over the ground. Mr Scott said afterwards that it was the most entertaining junior football game he had ever watched.

Fox was sure that Miles Winter would have approached the Birdman to play for the Dragons because he was such a talented footballer, but the Stingrays captain had obviously said no, which made Fox like him even more.

The final against the Stonewarren Stingrays turned out to be a seesawing affair. With all their best players on the field, the Diggers dominated the game—but as soon as several of their key players were placed on the bench, the Stingrays would come back.

The game was once again highlighted by the spectacular marking of the Birdman and Fox. In the second quarter, the Birdman flew over Mo and Bruno and sat perched on their shoulders for what seemed liked seconds before taking a mighty grab.

Mo got up, dusted himself off and said to the Birdman, "Thawozapurteekulgramuh," which Paige kindly translated as, "That was a pretty cool grab, mate."

"Thanks!" said the the Birdman, with a cheeky grin.

Less than a minute later, Fox stood on the head of the Stingrays' centre half-back and brought down an absolute hanger. To cap it off, he landed on his feet, played on, baulked around an opponent, and kicked a drop punt straight over the goal umpire's head.

Lewis ran out to Fox and said in a Scottish accent, "Fooks! That was mooch better than seeing the Loch Ness monsta, laddie—but don't tell Nessie I said that, 'cause she can be a bit sensitive!"

In the end, the Diggers had more players capable of kicking goals, and this proved to be the difference between the two teams. Fox kicked four, Simon kicked four, Paige kicked three, and Chase and Jimmy kicked two each.

The final scoreboard read:

Diggers   15.6 (96)
Visitors   10.15 (75)

Fox was absolutely thrilled to win as it meant they had another chance to knock off the Dragons. Unfortunately, based on last week's game the Diggers had about as much chance of winning the match as Vince did of becoming a nuclear scientist.

That night Miles received another email from Mr Jackson.

Dear Miles,

I am once again writing to you on behalf of the parents of the Dragons recruits. We wish to inform you that if you want our boys to play in the Grand Final you will need to pay us a "Grand Final Bonus" of $150 per player on top of the "Finals Bonus" of $100 per player. There should also be an added bonus to the bonus incentive scheme so that players are to be paid $50 for each goal they kick, and an extra $200 if they are named in the best players.

If you refuse this request, the boys will come down with a sudden case of "gastro" and will not be able to play.

I look forward to hearing back from you.

Have a nice day,

Mark Jackson

"These guys are bloodsuckers!" thought Miles furiously. "But I guess the bonus system did work well in the first final—if I pay them more, we'll probably thrash the Diggers by 20 goals in the Grand Final."

So he typed:

No problemo.

Miles then made a quick note in his diary to visit Mr Shloogal at the bank and take out some more money from the Tilley Fawcett Inheritance Trust Account.

He leaned back in his chair in the study and thought, "When we crush the Diggers next week I will finally get my vengeance on the Swifts for all the horrible things they've done to me."

Then, after letting out a loud sigh of satisfaction, Miles turned off the study light and went to bed.

16

Goal Hungry

On the day of the Grand Final, Fox woke early and headed to the kitchen.

Chase was already sitting at the table eating a bowl of cereal. Fox marvelled at his little brother's ability to make a mess out of even the simplest of tasks.

"The aim is to pour the milk *into* the bowl," said Fox with a grin.

Chase looked down at the large pool of milk on the table.

"Guess there's no use crying over spilt milk!" he said, and then burst out laughing.

Mr Swift walked in and stared at the milky mess.

"Chase, how is it that you never miss a goal, but you always miss your bowl?"

"Hey Dad, that's a rhyme!" said Chase.

"Here's another one: move your cup and mop it up!" said Mr Swift, throwing a cloth that hit Chase in the head.

"Morning!" said Mrs Swift as she entered the kitchen.

"Morning, Mum," said Fox.

"Mrningmumph," said Chase with a mouth full of cereal.

"You sound just like Mo," said Mr Swift.

This was a big mistake, as it caused Chase to erupt with laughter. Milk and cereal exploded from his mouth and went everywhere.

"Chase! I nearly lost an eye!" complained Mr Swift.

"You made me laugh, so you have to clean it up," said Chase, throwing the cloth back at his dad.

"Me?! You made the mess! How about we let your mother decide?"

Mr Swift and Chase then put on their cutest puppy-dog faces and stared at Mrs Swift.

"Awww, you both look so cute—so you can both clean it up!"

Fox laughed and tossed another cloth at Chase. It was pretty hard to be nervous about a Grand Final when your family was such an entertaining distraction.

Mr Scott pulled out a brilliant surprise just before the start of the game.

"Cyril Rioli really wanted to be here with you today," he said, "so we talked about getting him to send you a Skype message—"

"That is so cool—a Skype message from Cyril!" said Rosie as everyone cheered.

"Unfortunately, I didn't know how to use Skype—"

There was a loud, collective "Awww" of disappointment.

"So instead—Cyril decided to come here in person!"

With that, Cyril walked into the changing rooms. The Diggers were stunned.

"No way!" said Hugo.

"Yes way!" said Fox.

"On ya, cuz!" yelled out Lewis.

The players gave a huge round of applause for the AFL star, and Fox could already sense the boost Cyril's presence had given the team.

A hush fell over the changing room as Cyril cleared his throat to speak. No one wanted to miss a word he said.

"I want you to remember one thing," said Cyril. "A champion team will always beat a team of champions."

"That's right!" yelled out Bruno.

"While I was waiting for Mr Scott to signal for me to walk in, I was listening at the door. I heard you guys talking to each other, encouraging each other—that's what a real team does. And you know what?"

"What?" called out Lewis.

"I did not hear one sound coming out of next door. The Dragons may be a great side on paper, but they don't sound like a great team to me. If you guys can stick at it and put some pressure on them, they will fold—because when the going gets tough, they won't play for each other like you guys will play for each other. I believe you guys are a real team and I know you can go out there and win today. Remember, this is the last game of the season, so put everything into it because there is no 'next week'!"

Fox stood up. He had never been so pumped before a game in all his life.

"Come on, Diggers!" he yelled.

Every teammate responded with "Come on!" as Fox led them out the door.

Joey and Gary escorted the team on to the oval and the crowd gave them a noisy and uplifting reception. Even though the match was once again being played at the Dragons' home ground, the Diggers fans were definitely in the majority.

Matilda Wall, Snowy Davison and Mr Scott's friend Samantha Lu were standing with the parents and siblings of the Diggers players.

Fox spotted the policeman, Lex Hunt, in the crowd and noticed he was wearing a Diggers scarf.

"After meeting Mace, he probably decided to barrack for whoever was playing against the Dragons!" he thought.

Nearby stood Miss Carey, who was wearing a T-shirt with the words "Run-DMC" on it. She wore runners without shoelaces and was listening and singing along to a tiny MP3 player: "Walk this way, talk this way, well just give me a kiss ..."

"Oh my God," said Lewis. "That was like the only cool song from the last century, and she has completely ruined it for me!"

Mr Percy was also there, and on the front of his T-shirt were the words "(Unofficial) Diggers Coach". The word "Unofficial" was tiny, and could only be seen up close.

Chase thought this was pretty funny until Lewis said, "Wait 'til you see the back of his T-shirt!"

Mr Percy turned around and Chase was horrified to read the words: "I taught Chase and Jimmy everything they know".

Chase looked at Jimmy and said, "Not cool, dude, not cool!"

All around the oval were men and women and boys and girls decked out in yellow and blue.

"Let's give our supporters something to cheer about today!" said Fox.

The Dragons then came out on to the ground and burst through a giant specially made banner that Miles Winter had spent a lot of money on.

The message on the banner summed up the cockiness of the Dragons in a few words. It said, "This flag is in the bag—go the undefeated Unbeatables".

On the other side was an ad for Miles' legal business. It was supposed to say, "As lawyers go, Miles Winter is one cool dude". Unfortunately, the 'e' had fallen off the banner so it read, "As lawyers go, Miles Winter is one cool dud".

Fox walked around his teammates as they warmed up and gave words of encouragement to every single one of them. "Lots of leading from you, Simon; you'll get a lot of crumbs today, Paige; run them into the ground, Rosie; don't give them a sniff, Bruno; they won't be able to tackle you, Chung; you're going to kill them in the middle, Sammy; use your height up forward, Chris …"

He heard a blast of the whistle and knew it was time for the toss.

Fox was delighted to see that Mr Bigg was again in charge of their match. Not only was he an excellent umpire, but he also didn't put up with any of Mace's nonsense.

"You're the away captain again, Fox," said Mr Bigg, "so what will it be—heads or tails?"

"Tails," Fox said a little half-heartedly as the coin

was launched into the air. He was thinking about his abysmal strike rate when it came to winning the toss.

"And … tails it is!" said the umpire.

Fox couldn't believe it.

He quickly pointed to the end he wanted the Diggers to kick to, and Mr Bigg said, "Now I want you both to shake hands."

Mace didn't want to shake hands with Fox, but he also didn't want to give away a goal like he'd done last time. He grudgingly shook Fox's hand, then leaned in close and whispered something very rude into the Diggers captain's ear.

"What was that?!" asked Mr Bigg

"I just said, 'Best of luck'," said Mace.

This wasn't what Fox had heard, but he politely said, "And the same to you" anyway.

Miles spotted Mo Officer running to the bench at the start of the first quarter and breathed a sigh of relief. He had been worried that Mr Scott might play his best team for the whole game in the Grand Final, which would have spelt danger for the Dragons.

"Mr Scott really is a loser," thought Miles. "Sandy will kick at least four goals from full-forward in the first quarter."

The Grand Final started off in much the same way as the previous final had, with the Dragons taking advantage of Mo's absence and Sandy Barr scoring the four goals predicted by Miles.

On the plus side, Chris and Sammy dominated in the ruck and Fox picked up an enormous number of possessions in the middle of the ground. But every time the Dragons won the ball they kicked it to a teammate who was playing on a less talented opponent. For example, Hugo was playing on the former Romana Roosters star Peter 'Roady' Rodan. Time and time again the Dragons would kick the ball to Roady, who would outmark Hugo, then dodge around him and send a pass to Sandy on the lead.

At quarter-time the scoreboard read:

Dragons   6.5 (41)
Visitors   3.1 (19)

In the quarter-time huddle Miles warned his players that anyone who slackened off would be dragged straight away.

"Hopefully that loser Mr Scott will be resting Bruno this quarter, and, if so, that means you have to kick the ball to Jacko whenever we enter the forward line."

When Miles saw Bruno heading to the boundary at the start of the second quarter, he knew the game was all but over.

"Without their star centre half-back, Jacko will dominate!" he thought.

He began to imagine what his name would look like

on the honour board in the Dragons' clubrooms.

The second quarter followed a similar pattern to the first—the only difference being that instead of Sandy kicking most of the Dragons' goals, it was Jacko. Fox continued to star in the midfield, Paige kicked a spectacular left-foot goal (which she followed up with some equally spectacular cartwheels) and Rosie never stopped running. Chung used his speed and evasiveness to great advantage, and Fox was very impressed at how much his new friend's kicking and handball skills had improved over the season. Chase and Jimmy threw themselves into every contest despite the fact they were playing on opponents much bigger than themselves.

This quarter Hugo was playing on the former Tennant Hill Tigers star Tony 'Lightning' Lucas. Tony was very skilful and very fast, and he ran rings around Hugo for the entire quarter.

Hugo was desperately trying to think of a way to help his side when an idea came to him.

He turned to Tony and said, "Hey Lightning, is the rumour true about Jacko?"

"What rumour?" asked Lightning.

"That his dad told him to kick as many goals as he can and not to give any away."

"What?"

"Something about maximising his bonus?"

"Jacko's not like that, he'd never—"

But just as Lightning was saying this, he saw Jacko, who had the chance to shepherd a teammate's kick through for a goal, grab the ball and kick the goal himself.

"That lowdown dirty bonus thief!" he cried.

Seconds later, the half-time siren sounded and Lightning immediately rushed over to Jacko and started screaming at him. "I know what you're up to and there is no way you're getting another pass from me all day!"

"What's going on?" asked Roady, who had come over to see what his teammates were arguing about.

"Jacko's just trying to kick as many goals as he can— he doesn't give a stuff about the rest of us!" Lightning said accusingly.

"Is that true, Jacko?" asked Roady.

"No way!" said Jacko.

Unfortunately for Jacko, his dad chose that exact moment to yell out, "Good on you, son—at this rate we'll be able to get a spa put in the backyard!"

Fox watched on as the Dragons players continued bickering all the way to the changing rooms.

"I wonder what that's all about," thought Fox.

But he didn't really have time to think about it, because the scoreboard was telling him the Diggers were in big trouble:

Dragons   15.8 (98)
Visitors   7.2 (44)

The Dragons were in front by 54 points!

Even though the Dragons players were arguing in the changing rooms at half-time, Miles Winter had never been happier. His team led by nine goals! And better still, Fox Swift, Paige Turner, Sammy and Simon 'Porky' Phillips were still to be subbed off by Mr Scott.

"This is soooo sweet!" he thought.

Over in the Diggers' changing rooms, Mr Scott was still as positive as ever. "Fantastic effort there, Diggers. Get your breath back, have a drink to replace your fluids, and don't think we are out of this by any means."

Fox went around to his teammates reminding them of the good things they had done in the first half. He was desperate to help turn the game around, but he knew it was his turn to have a quarter on the bench.

"Okay," said Mr Scott, "we need to rest a few of you this quarter to make sure everyone gets a go—"

The coach was interrupted by Hugo putting up his hand and saying, "Mr Scott, my hamstring is a little tight, so I'd better come off the ground."

"Really? Well, okay then, Hugo—"

Then another of the less talented Diggers players put up his hand. "My calf muscle has been playing up a bit," said Noel Green, "I better come off, too."

One by one, the less skilful Diggers players were struck by sudden injuries and/or illnesses. The most interesting one was Paul Whitford, who said he was pretty sure he had come down with a bout of rabies.

Mr Scott suspected his players were inventing their afflictions, but it was their decision and he had to respect that. He could hardly force them to play against their will.

Just before the start of the third quarter, Miles looked over at the Diggers' bench and started to panic.

He had expected to see Fox sitting down, or at least Paige, Chris and Sammy, but none of them were there. It looked like the Diggers had their best possible team on the field.

"Nine goals—we can't lose when we have a lead of nine goals," he said, trying to calm himself down.

Less than a minute into the quarter, Fox kicked a long goal after weaving in and out of four Dragons players.

"Eight goals—we can't lose when we have a lead of eight goals," Miles said to himself.

An outbreak of infighting among the Dragons players greatly assisted the chances of a Diggers comeback. When Lightning Lucas ran past Jacko on the way to goal calling for a handball, Jacko ignored him and took the shot himself for a behind.

"You idiot, Jacko!" said Lightning. "You just cost me $50!" From then on the Dragons became more and more selfish. They paid no attention to leads from their teammates and attempted goals from impossible angles.

Handballs in the forward line became non-existent as everyone tried to pick up the $50 bonus for scoring a goal.

Miles started to chew his fingernails as he said to himself, "Six goals—we can't lose when we have a lead of six goals."

At three-quarter time, Fox looked over at the scoreboard and was surprised to see how much the Diggers had closed the gap.

Dragons	16.17 (113)
Visitors	13.7 (85)

"Twenty-eight points," he thought. "We can do this!"

Mr Scott gave a rousing speech to the Diggers in the huddle.

"You have one quarter of the entire season left—are you going to give it everything you've got?"

"YES!" yelled the Diggers.

"That was a fantastic effort in the third quarter and I'm going to need that from you again—can you give it to me?"

"YES!"

"Are you going to keep on running and never give up?"

"YES!"

"Are you going to win this game for your supporters and each other?"

"YES!"

In the other huddle, Mr Winter was panicking. Hearing the enthusiastic Diggers yelling out "YES!" made him even more nervous.

In desperation, he tried to imitate Mr Scott.

"Are we going to win?" he said.

But most of the players simply shrugged their shoulders, and Roady just said, "Meh."

"Twenty-eight points—we can't lose when we have a lead of 28 points," thought Mr Winter.

The fourth and final quarter started off well for the Diggers, with Sammy palming the ball to Fox, who handballed to Chung, who handballed to Rosie, who burst through the centre and kicked a beautiful long pass to Chase.

There was enormous pressure on the young Digger, but Fox watched his brother take his run-up and slot the goal, as cool as one of Mr Percy's giant cucumbers.

Dragons   16.17 (113)
Visitors   14.7 (91)

At the next centre bounce, Chris thumped the ball 30 metres into the forward line and Paige swooped on it and then speared a beautiful pass straight on to Simon's chest.

Simon went back, pulled up his socks and picked out an object behind the two big sticks to aim at. With his perfect kicking technique, he made no mistake.

Dragons   16.17 (113)
Visitors   15.7 (97)

To the Dragons' credit, they started to fight much harder. Many of their players were competitive by nature and they really didn't want to lose. None more so than Mace, who Fox had to admit was playing very well.

Roady and Lightning both scored goals for the Dragons, but the Diggers hit back hard with goals from Sammy, Paige and Rosie followed by an incredible left-foot snap from the boundary by Fox.

Dragons   18.19 (127)
Visitors   19.10 (124)

With only a few minutes to go and the Diggers trailing by just three points, the ball was in the Diggers' forward line when Jimmy Rioli was crunched by Mace in a tackle. The knock completely winded him, and Lewis helped his brave younger brother off the ground.

Mr Scott looked at the players on the bench. "Hugo, you're on."

"Me?" said Hugo.

"Yep. After all, you won us the Grand Final last year—and I believe you can do it again."

It meant a lot for Hugo to hear that his coach still had confidence in him, and he raced on to the field and positioned himself in the forward pocket, determined to do his best.

With the clock ticking down, Vince was awarded a free kick at centre half-back. Mace had snuck out to his left and all Vince needed to do was make a short **chip kick** and his captain would be away. Luckily for the Diggers, Sammy was on the mark, and because he was so tall he managed to intercept the pass. As Vince went to tackle him, Sammy shot a quick, high kick deep into the Diggers' forward line.

… Where the only player left was Hugo! No one from the Dragons had bothered to pick him up, leaving him wide open.

Hugo kept his eyes locked on the ball as it came down towards him. The crowd held its breath.

Hugo went to take the mark on his chest, and as he leapt into the air he was sure he had it covered. But he was wrong.

"Falcon!" yelled Mace as the ball thumped Hugo on the head. Mace was laughing so hard he nearly fell over.

But while nearly every player on the ground had stopped to watch these events unfold, Chase had started running. At training, Mr Scott had told them repeatedly to always "Run to help out your teammates—you never know when they might make a mistake or need to give you a handball." And Chase was doing exactly that.

The ball had hit Hugo so hard on the head that it had bounced off into the air and flown about 15 metres away near the goalsquare. Chase swooped on it before it hit the ground, then ran into the open goal and snapped one through to put the Diggers three points up!

Dragons	18.19 (127)	
Visitors	20.10 (130)	

A huge roar erupted from the crowd, car horns sounded and Diggers players ran from everywhere to congratulate Chase.

Lewis ran on to the ground and yelled, "That was the best **goal assist** ever, Hugo! 'Dangerman' strikes again!"

This made Hugo feel a lot better, especially because Lewis had used the nickname Hugo had (unsuccessfully) tried to give himself the year before. Lewis then ran over to Fox and said, "I just spoke to the timekeeper—there is a minute and 15 seconds to go."

Before Mr Bigg bounced the ball to restart play, Fox gathered Sammy, Rosie and Chung in the middle of the ground.

"Okay guys, there's just over a minute to go. Sammy, I want you to palm the ball to Chung, and Chung, when you get the ball I want you to run—run and bounce the ball and don't get tackled. If you can do that for a minute, we win the game."

With Fox's plan in mind, Sammy palmed the centre bounce straight to Chung, who took off like a flash, zigzagging, propping and sidestepping. Chung ran from one side of the ground to the other, spinning and weaving his way out of trouble—it seemed like the entire Dragons team was chasing after him, but no one could catch him.

Watching Chung's incredible evasive skills from the boundary, Miles started to turn a deep shade of purple.

With only 20 seconds remaining, the Dragons players had all but given up—Chung was just too good. That's when Miles noticed a three-year-old boy kicking a plastic footy next to him on the boundary. Miles quickly stole the footy and booted it on to the field so that it landed right next to Mr Bigg.

Mr Bigg immediately blew his whistle to signal the timekeeper to stop the clock. He gave a stern look in the direction the ball had come from. Miles motioned his head towards the little boy and mouthed, "It was him," prompting the three-year-old to march over and give Miles an almighty kick in the shin.

Mr Bigg said, "Sorry Chung, I don't have a choice— hand me back the footy. I have to ball it up."

The Diggers players and fans couldn't believe what was happening. To make matters worse, neither Sammy nor Chris was anywhere near where the ball was being thrown up, which meant the Dragons ruckman was able to go up unopposed and win his first knock for the day.

The ball was kicked forward by Roady and then picked up by Vince on the **half-volley**. Mace screamed for the handball but Vince ignored him, turned on to his right foot and snapped a goal. The siren sounded less than a second later.

Dragons	19.19 (133)
Visitors	20.10 (130)

The Dragons had won by three points.

17

Hero to Zero

Vince assumed that Mace would be over the moon with the Dragons' victory, but he was wrong.

"Why didn't you handball it to me?" screamed Mace.

"But I just won us the game," said Vince.

"Oh, it's all about you, isn't it! You are so selfish," said Mace.

Mace's father was a lot more excited. He ran over to where Fox's parents were standing and cried, "I did it! I won!"

"Who says there's no 'I' in team?" said Mr Swift.

"Nice to see you being so humble in victory, Miles," said Mrs Swift.

"Who's being the bad sport now?" snapped Miles.

"I'm pretty sure you are," said Mr Swift.

"Well, I can be, because I'm a winner—a W-I-N-E-R!"

"A 'winer'?" said Mrs Swift. "Well, I guess you do

whine quite a bit, so—"

"I don't care what you say—I beat you losers fair and square and there's nothing you can do to take that away from me. Nothing. Ha!"

Miles ran off punching the air and singing an old song by Queen called *We Are the Champions*—except he changed the words slightly so it went, "I am the champion, my friends ..."

"Friends?" said Mr Swift, acting surprised. "Miles has friends?"

Fox was devastated to lose to the Dragons, but he was also incredibly proud of the way his teammates had worked together all day and of their tireless efforts to come back. They had been so close to snatching victory.

He went around shaking the Dragons players' hands and trying to comfort his teammates.

Lewis ran out and tried to cheer Fox up by putting on his Scottish accent.

"Fooks Swift! Well done laddie, aye. You were mugnificent oot there! You did all ya could, aye? Ya kicked gools, ya took hungers, and ya played with heart! You've made ya clan vury proode, Fooks Swift!"

Even though they had won the Grand Final, the mood in the Dragons' post-game huddle was quite flat.

"So who were the best players?" demanded Mr Jackson, and the other parents nodded—they all wanted to know if their son would receive a "best player" bonus.

Now that the Dragons had won, Miles didn't care about upsetting the parents. So he came up with his "3-2-1" votes based purely on what would save him the most money.

"Today I give one vote to Vince—"

"What?!" yelled out Peter Rodan's dad.

"Well, he did kick the winning goal," Miles replied smoothly.

"Two votes go to ... Mace. Great game, son!"

"Giving your own son two votes—what a surprise!" yelled out Tony Lucas' father.

"It is a surprise," said Mr Jackson. "I thought he'd give him three votes!"

"And the three votes go to someone who kept calm all day while everyone else was panicking ..."

Mr Jackson, Mr Lucas and Mr Rodan waited expectantly, each one confident that Miles was describing his son.

"Yes, without a doubt the most valuable contributor to the Dragons today was ... me!"

"What?!" cried Mr Jackson.

"You have got to be joking!" yelled Mr Rodan.

"No, the joke's on you lot," said Miles, "because I can finally tell you what I really think of you. I have waited so long to get this off my chest! You are a pack of bloodsucking leeches. I hate every single one of you and I am not paying your sons another cent!"

It was right at this moment that the umpire, Mr Bigg, walked into the Dragons' huddle. He had come over to congratulate the players on their win.

"Did I just hear you say you've been paying your players, Mr Winter?" asked Mr Bigg.

The angry mob went silent and waited for Miles to answer.

"Um, no, of course not ..."

"Liar!" yelled out Mr Jackson.

"Yeah, he paid my son," said Mr. Rodan.

"And mine—out of something called the Tilley Fawcett Inheritance Trust Account," said Mr Lucas, who had noticed the unusual name on one of Miles' cheques. He had given Miles the benefit of the doubt at the time, but given his recent behaviour, Mr Lucas now suspected foul play.

Sergeant Lex Hunt, who had come over to see what all the commotion was about, walked over to Mr Lucas and said, "Did you say Miles paid you out of the Tilley Fawcett Inheritance Trust Account?"

"Yep, I've even got a copy of one of the cheques at home."

"Hmm," thought Sergeant Hunt, taking out his phone.

Meanwhile, back in the Diggers' huddle, Mr Scott was giving his final address of the season.

"Congratulations on a brilliant team effort this year. Every single one of you is a better footballer than at the start of the season—and that's the most important thing. I know you are all disappointed about today's result, but it was a fantastic game, and even though you came up just short, you should be very proud."

The players and supporters all clapped.

"I want to thank you all for having me as a coach. I am so lucky to be in this position—"

"I'll say!" called out Mr Percy.

When everyone laughed, Mr Percy said, "I wasn't joking, people!"

"As I was saying," Mr Scott went on, "even though we didn't win today—"

Mr Scott was interrupted by the crackle of the PA system.

Everyone turned to see where the noise was coming from and spotted Mr Bigg standing on a chair next to the scoreboard holding a microphone.

"Ladies and gentlemen, I have a very important announcement to make," he said.

"What's going on?" asked Chase.

Fox shrugged his shoulders.

"It has come to my attention," said Mr Bigg, "that the Dragons have been paying their players. This is absolutely against the rules and as a result they have been disqualified from the competition. That means ... the Diggers are the official premiers!"

"You little bewdy!" yelled Lewis as all the Diggers supporters started cheering and jumping up and down.

On the other side of the ground, most of the Dragons players and supporters didn't seem to care, except for Miles, who went down on his knees and screamed, "Nooooooooooooooooooooooooooooooooooooo!"

Fox watched Mr Scott give Joey and Samantha Lu a huge hug. He had never seen his coach look happier.

He saw Chung talking excitedly with Cyril Rioli about his incredible weaving run at the very end of the final quarter. Chung grinned from ear to ear when the Hawthorn star said, "You took the game on, Chung, and that's what it's all about!"

Fox then went over to where Chase and Jimmy were standing, with Gary the rabbit running in between and around their legs. It seemed as though Gary was just as excited as everyone else.

"That was a big hit you took, Jimmy—how are you feeling?" asked Fox.

"Now that we've won, really good!" said Jimmy, beaming.

"You two were great today."

"Yeah, we were," said Chase. "… Just kidding!"

Fox was about to say something else when all of a sudden he was flying through the air. Sammy and Chris had picked him up and put him on their shoulders.

"Lucky you're not afraid of heights!" called out Lewis.

From his vantage point on top of his mates' shoulders, Fox judged that the most excited Diggers supporter was Chung's father.

Mr Lee pushed his way into the middle of the huddle, did a small dance and announced, "Free food at Feng's Way tonight!" Everyone cheered and started jumping up and down again.

When he had climbed off their shoulders, Fox gave Sammy and Chris a hug. "You guys are the best," he said, giving them both a knuckle-punch.

He wandered over to Hugo, who was looking a bit sad.

"Hey Hugo, what's up? Did Amanda just give Bruno a hug?"

"No, I'm totally cool with that now," said Hugo. "Bruno's a great guy, so I'm glad my sister is dating him."

"Then what's going on?"

"I feel like I let the team down today—and I got falconed again!" he said glumly.

"No way, Hugo! I heard you were the one who caused the Dragons to start fighting with each other."

"Yeah, that was me," said Hugo, with a sly smile.

"That's what turned the game our way after half-time," said Fox. "And it was your falcon that set up Chase for an important goal. So, in a way, it was less of a falcon and more like an accidental header—like the soccer players do!"

"I guess so," grinned Hugo.

"So if I was choosing the best players, you would definitely be on my list."

"Thanks heaps, Fox," said Hugo, suddenly feeling a lot better.

In among the celebrations, Lewis dashed over and changed the scoreboard to reflect the true scores.

| Dragons | 0.0 (0) |
| Visitors | 20.10 (130) |

Miles fled the Dragons parents, who were still demanding money, and stormed off towards his sports car. He was so mad he once again snatched the plastic football away from the three-year-old kid and tried to kick it as far away as he could.

Unfortunately, Miles slipped as he kicked it and

landed flat on his backside. There was a loud burst of laughter from Mr and Mrs Swift and some of the other Diggers parents.

To add insult to injury, the little kid grabbed his footy back, threw it up into the air and took a specky on Miles as he lay on the ground.

Mr and Mrs Swift almost fell down laughing.

"Don't you dare laugh at me!" shouted Miles as Mace and Vince helped him to his feet. "I'm about to jump into my very expensive car and drive off to my nice big mansion, while you pack of losers—"

"No, you're not. You're coming with me," said Sergeant Hunt, marching over authoritatively.

"What for?" cried Mr Winter.

"For using money that doesn't belong to you," said Sergeant Hunt.

"I don't know what you're talking about!"

"Does the Tilley Fawcett Inheritance Trust Account ring any bells?"

"Um, err ... I can assure you that was all above board."

"Yeah!" said Vince, jumping to Mr Winter's defence. "Just because he paid the parents in the laneway, wearing a false beard and a wig, doesn't mean he's guilty."

"Shut up, Vince!"

"Come with me please, Mr Winter," said Sergeant Hunt.

"We have to do something," whispered Mace. "I know! I'll offer him a bribe."

"Good idea," whispered Vince.

"You know, Sergeant Hunt, there is a lot of money in that account—if you know what I mean?" said Mace, with a very obvious wink.

"Are you trying to bribe me?" Sergeant Hunt said sternly.

Mace sensed he had made a mistake and was about to backpedal and deny the accusation when Vince chimed in with, "He sure is, sergeant!"

"Shut up, Vince!"

"You really think you can get out of this by offering me money?" asked the sergeant.

"If you don't want money, I've got some really rare footy cards," said Vince.

"All three of you are coming with me!" said Sergeant Hunt.

As they walked past the Diggers, Lewis said to Miles, "If you want some decent legal advice, you really should hire Hugo!"

Lewis handed Miles a funny business card he had drawn up with Hugo's name on it. Miles went bright red, screwed up the bit of paper and threw it on the ground.

"Remind me to also fine you for littering," said Sergeant Hunt.

MR HUGO TRIPPITT
Legal Eagle
1800 - LEGEND

As they were walking towards the police car, Miles again pleaded his innocence. "I swear the Tilley Fawcett Inheritance Trust Account is all above board—I tried to find Tilley Fawcett but she doesn't exist."

"Oh yes she does," replied the policeman. "In fact, she's at the game today."

"What?" said Miles. "Where?"

Sergeant Hunt pointed to a woman who was talking to Snowy Davison while her pet rabbit ran around her feet. It was Matilda Wall.

"Before she was married her name was Matilda Fawcett, but everyone called her 'Tilley'," explained Sergeant Hunt. "Back then, she was a trained nurse and she took great care of her neighbour Beverly

Stephenson when she was sick. Ms Stephenson never forgot her kindness, which is why she left all her money to Tilley."

A minute later, the Diggers supporters watched the divvy van drive away with Miles, Mace and Vince in the back.

Judge Trudy Binding was shocked when she heard about Miles using money out of the Tilley Fawcett Inheritance Trust Account, and she ordered him to repay every cent of it immediately.

"Unfortunately I have a slight cash-flow problem at the moment and I won't be able to pay back Mrs Fawcett for the next, uh, 20 years or so," Mr Winter told the court.

"But I could be dead by then!" called out Matilda.

"Mr Winter, you will either pay the money now or hand over assets to Ms Fawcett to the value of the amount you owe her," said Judge Trudy.

"But the only asset I actually own outright is my home," said Miles. "I'm still paying the mortgage on my rentals."

"That makes it nice and easy, then," said Judge Trudy. "Ms Fawcett, Mr Winter's home is now yours. Mr Winter, have the papers drawn up and signed by the end of the day."

"But, but, but—" stammered Miles.

But it was too late. Judge Trudy banged her gavel and the case was over. Miles could not believe the old lady he had once evicted was now evicting him!

Fox Swift cut the clipping out of the *Davinal Digest* and stuck it into his scrapbook.

U-13 Grand Final
Davinal Diggers 20.10 (130) **d** Davinal Dragons 0.0 (0)

Diggers Best: F. Swift (B.O.G.), R. McHusky, R. Officer, P. Turner, C. Wek, S. Saaed, B. Gallucci, C. Lee, S. Phillips, C. Swift, J. Rioli

Diggers Goals: F. Swift 5, S. Phillips 3, P. Turner 3, C. Swift 3, J. Rioli 2, R. McHusky 1, C. Lee 1, C. Wek 1, S. Saaed 1
Dragons Best: -
Dragons Goals: -

It had been an amazing year for the Diggers. The side had been made even stronger with the inclusion of Rosie and Chung, and even though the season had just finished, Fox couldn't wait for the next one to start.

Just then, Chase walked into Fox's room holding a footy. "Cool," he said, looking at the two premiership photos on Fox's wall.

PEEKING
PERCY

"If you look closely, you can see that Mr Percy managed to sneak into the back of this year's picture too," said Fox. Chase laughed, and then a serious look came over his face. "Hey, I wonder what dirty tricks Mace will have up his sleeve next year?"

"Maybe he's learned his lesson and he'll be really nice," said Fox.

There was a slight pause before they both burst out laughing.

As part of their punishment for the player-payments scandal and attempting to bribe a police officer, Miles, Mace and Vince were ordered to do community service.

This involved picking up rubbish along the side of the highway on Saturday afternoons. To make things even worse, they had to wear orange jumpsuits with "Correctional Community Service Workers" on the back.

"This is so humiliating," said Miles, as he picked up a dirty nappy that had been tossed on the side of the road. He screwed up his nose in disgust as he placed it in a giant garbage bag.

Suddenly a car drove by and a passenger threw a half-full milkshake out the window. It hit Miles on the chest, then burst open and covered all three of them with sticky liquid.

"What was that?!" screamed Miles.

"Mmm," said Vince, licking his lips. "I think it's banana flavour—"

"Shut up, Vince!" yelled Mace and Miles together.

Mace was furious. The Dragons had been suspended from the League, he was wearing an orange jumpsuit and he was covered in banana-flavoured milk.

"You'll pay for this, Swift—you will so pay for this!" he vowed.

A Quirky Footy Dictionary

Baulk—means hesitate or pull back from something. For example, your parents will sometimes baulk at buying you a new set of football boots when they see the price tag. Baulking someone on the footy field means avoiding or getting around them—you make them think you are going to go one way, and then you go the other. The best thing about the word 'baulk' is if you say it quickly over and over, you sound like a chicken. (Warning: If you start doing this in public, people might think you're crazy and start baulking you.)

Bicycle kick—a goal scored with a bicycle kick does not mean a goal kicked by a half-forward flanker on a BMX. This spectacular type of goal occurs when a player facing away from the goals leaps up, somersaults in mid-air and kicks the ball back over his or her head. At the time of kicking the ball, the player is actually upside down. Calling this a bicycle kick is weird, though, as the only thing harder than kicking a ball when you're pedalling is riding your bike upside down.

Bush star—someone who plays well on ovals covered in shrubs. Not really. A bush star is a champion (star) footballer who plays for a country team, i.e. out in the bush. (If your oval *is* covered in shrubs, it's probably time to get a new groundskeeper!)

Chest mark—a chest mark is where a player takes a mark by wrapping their arms around the ball just as it hits them on the chest. This is the safest way to take a mark, especially in the wet. Chest marking is easier if you have a really, really hairy chest because the hair acts as a kind of net—however, it's very embarrassing when the ball gets stuck in a player's chest hair and the umpire has to call time on to go fetch some scissors. Ouch!

Chip kick—this is when you lob the footy over an opponent's head into the arms of your teammate. It is very difficult to do—next time someone offers you a chip, instead of eating it, try to kick it and you will see for yourself. But be careful when kicking a chicken chip, or you might end up with egg on your face!

Close-checking—when you are doing a maths test and a really annoying teacher stands behind you and watches as you answer the questions, that is an example of close-checking. (And don't you hate it when the teacher does a loud sigh after you write an answer?!) On the football field, if you have an opposition player who is constantly looking over your shoulder, breathing down your neck and generally being annoying, then they are called a close-checking opponent.

Contested ball—this where the ball is not in anyone's possession and you and an opposition player are both going for it. Whoever emerges with the footy has won the 'contested ball'. Not to be confused with a 'congested ball', which is a footy that has the sniffles.

Corridor—attacking 'down the corridor' means kicking and running the ball through the middle of the oval, not wasting time by going out wide to the flanks. At home, 'corridor football' means kicking the ball down the hallway. This is usually followed by three things: marks on the walls, a broken lamp and kids being grounded.

Deck—a ball 'hitting the deck' simply means it hits the ground. Unless of course you are on a ship, and then it means it's going to really annoy the people sun-baking on the banana lounges. (Warning: 'Deck' can sound like a rude word when spoken by a New Zealander.)

Dished off—this is where you quickly shoot off a handball to a teammate because you are about to be tackled. It is not where you pass a bowl to a teammate running by and ask them to stack it in a dishwasher for you. For starters, you should not be eating breakfast while on the field—that would make you a cereal offender.

Dragged—this is where the coach sends the runner out to take you from the ground because you are playing poorly. Some players refuse to come off and literally have to be dragged from the ground. This can be embarrassing, so remember, if you're being dragged, don't lag, be a dag or crack a gag, because you'll be bagged and your confidence will sag.

Draw an opponent—this is when you use the ball to make an opposition player leave their direct opponent (your teammate) and come to tackle you, so you can handball over their head to your teammate, who is now free—that is, you draw the player towards you like a magnet. I used to carry a small sketchpad in my sock so that if the coach said to me, "You did absolutely nothing that quarter!" I could pull out a sketch of a player and say, "Yes I did—I drew an opponent!"

Drilled—getting drilled when you go to the dentist is a bad thing: it means pain, a lot of gargling and a lecture about flossing. But on the footy field, if a player drills a pass at you it's a good thing: it means a low, fast pass that is hard to intercept.

Falcon—this is where a player is accidentally hit in the head with a footy. Personally, I think this is very unfair to falcons, which are a very coordinated type of bird. It also raises the question, if falcons get hit on the head by a footy, do they say, "I've been human-ed"?

Goal assist—when goalposts get old, they sometimes need a bit of help. If you ever see one at the lights, you should go over, put your arm around its waist and help it to cross the road: this is called a goal assist. When a player helps set up a goal—for example, by handballing the ball to a player who then kicks it through the big sticks—this is also called a goal assist.

Grab—this is another term for an overhead mark. It makes marking sound really easy, a bit like, "I'll just grab a grape from the fridge" or "I'll just grab a quick snooze". But the word 'grab' undersells just how difficult taking an overhead mark can be—"I ran at full speed towards a pack, pushed myself off an opponent's shoulders, launched myself metres into the air, stuck up my left arm and took a … grab." What an anticlimax!

Gun footballer—this is what they call a very good footballer. It is not a player who wanders around the field carrying a firearm. That would give a very different meaning to the phrase "having a shot for goal".

Half-volley—this is when you scoop up the ball a microsecond after it bounces. It's not a mark, because the ball has touched the ground, but if you gather the ball cleanly on the half-volley (which is not easy) it looks really cool! A word of warning: if you misjudge a half-volley, you can dislocate a finger, which is not cool at all!

Huddle—huddle rhymes with cuddle, and in a way a huddle is a group cuddle. This is where all the players get in really close and gather around each other at the end of a quarter to listen to the coach. You can always tell who has had a good quarter by where they stand in the huddle: footballers who have played a bad quarter tend to stand at the back of the huddle in order to avoid eye contact with the coach.

Left-footer—a player who kicks naturally with his or her left foot. About one in five players fall into this category. In the olden days, people who were left-handed were thought to be under the spell of the devil. And anyone who has ever played against a left-footer would have to agree—they are devilishly hard to tackle, because they turn a different way to right-footers when they go to kick. Famous left-footers include Dyson 'Hellboy' Heppell, Scott 'Prince of Darkness' Pendlebury and Buddy 'Beelzebub' Franklin.

Mark—this is the term for when a player catches a ball that has been kicked at least 15 metres without being touched by anyone. I can only assume that years ago there was some guy called Mark who was so good at catching the ball that someone said, "Hey, let's just call it a 'mark'." Commentators are pretty happy that this guy's name wasn't Mahershalalhashbaz.

Match time—means the amount of time players spend on the field during a match. It is traditional for parents of junior footballers to complain that their kids aren't getting enough match time whenever their child is taken off by the coach.

MCG, the—the Melbourne Cricket Ground, also known as the greatest sporting stadium in the history of the world, ever.* It is located in the heart of Melbourne and even though it has 'cricket' and not 'football' in its name, it is the official site of the AFL Grand Final every year.

*That may only be my opinion and not an actual fact. (Although in my opinion, it is a fact.)

Overhead mark—this is when you catch the ball with outstretched arms above your head. To mark overhead, you obviously need, a head—this is why the Headless Horseman, Headless Nick from Hogwarts and two of Henry VIII's six wives never played AFL footy.

Picked up—when you are told to go and pick up a

player you don't actually lift them up off the ground: that would be unfair, especially if you were asked to pick up a really heavy ruckman. And besides hurting your back, you'd probably give away a free kick for holding the man. When you are asked to 'pick up' a player it is your job is to make sure that whenever the opposition has the ball you are right alongside that player to try to stop them from getting it.

Rover—rovers are a bit like early explorers, in that they are allowed to go anywhere on the field they like. This sounds really cool, but the downside is they get blamed for everything. "Why weren't you there to help out the defenders?!" "Why weren't you there to crumb the ball in the forward pocket?!" "Why didn't you pick up your man in the middle of the ground?!" So to be a good rover it really helps to have a split personality or to master time travel—that way, you can be in three different spots at the same time, like the Doctor from *Doctor Who* ... and Gary Ablett.

Runner—the runner is the person who runs out on to the field and passes on messages from the coach to the players. Sometimes runners just come up to you and say, "Keep on doing what you're doing!" which I always found very strange—did they think I was about to lie down and have a nap for the rest of the quarter?

Sealer—this is not a goal kicked by that cheeky marine mammal or the English singer who used to appear on *The Voice*. A 'sealer' is the goal that is said to 'seal' the match—that is, after which there is no way the opposition could possibly come back and win as the margin is too great.

Seesawing battle—a match where one team leads for a little while, then the other team hits the front, then the other team gets back on top again. I think 'seesawing battle' is a pretty silly term as no one ever battles on a seesaw—can you imagine hopping on a seesaw, going up once then jumping off and saying, "I win! One-nil! In your face!"?

Seniors—this does not refer to a team of senior citizens zipping around an oval on mobility scooters, although I would definitely watch that. The senior team at a football club is made up of the best players in the club. If you are still eligible to play in a junior team but manage to make it into the senior team (like Mr Scott did), then you are a pretty talented young player!

Sherrin, the—the name of the manufacturer who makes footballs. Their name is boldly displayed on the ball. Some players are said to kick the ball so hard that when a teammate marks it, the word 'Sherrin' is imprinted on his or her chest!

Slot a major—to kick the ball into the gap (slot) between the big sticks and score a goal (a major). Slotting a major has nothing to do to with trying to post an army officer. In fact, I strongly recommend against this, as majors often have guns and tanks and should not be provoked.

Smothered—while it's a good thing to have your ice cream smothered in chocolate, it's not a good thing to have your kick smothered by an opponent. This is where your opponent uses his or her hands to block the ball just as it's leaving your boot. The only thing more embarrassing is being smothered in kisses by your mum in front of your mates at half-time.

Tagger—as well as being another name for someone who spray-paints their name on a wall, this is what they call a player who sticks very close to their opponent during a game. If you see an opponent running towards you with a can of spray paint in his or her sock, there is a good chance you are about to be tagged in one way or another—imagine looking down at your leg at quarter-time to find someone has spray-painted their initials on you and yelling, "OMG, I've been tagged!"

Throw a game—throwing games is difficult. Superman is one of the few people who could actually lift an oval and hurl it somewhere, so it's a good thing he plays American football and not Aussie Rules. To throw a game is to try to lose—it's where a player deliberately drops marks, gives away stupid free kicks and misses easy goals.

Wooden spooners—parents used to smack their children with a wooden spoon if they were naughty. Nowadays, teams are given the wooden spoon as punishment for coming last. After the last game of the season, the parents of the players in the bottom team are allowed to enter the changing rooms waving a wooden spoon and saying, "Don't do it again!" Due to the embarrassment caused by their parents displaying this kind of behaviour, AFL players in particular try to avoid coming last.

Wrong foot—putting your boots on the wrong feet makes it pretty hard to run and kick. On the plus side, it is very confusing for the opposition. Even more confusing is if you put your boots on backwards, so that they don't know if you're coming or going. But kicking the ball with your wrong foot means kicking with your non-preferred foot—so if you are a right-footer, it means kicking the ball with your left foot (and vice versa).

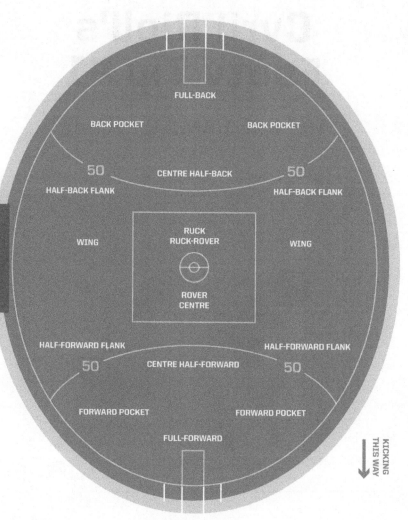

FULL-BACK

BACK POCKET · BACK POCKET

50 · CENTRE HALF-BACK · 50

HALF-BACK FLANK · HALF-BACK FLANK

INTERCHANGE BENCH

WING · RUCK RUCK-ROVER · WING

ROVER CENTRE

HALF-FORWARD FLANK · HALF-FORWARD FLANK

50 · CENTRE HALF-FORWARD · 50

FORWARD POCKET · FORWARD POCKET

FULL-FORWARD

KICKING THIS WAY

Cyril Rioli's Footy Tip #1

THE ONE-HANDED PICK-UP

Picking up the ball at speed is a real
crowd-pleaser and a team-lifter.

Keep your eye on the ball as you run towards it.

Plant your foot to the side of the ball and bend your knee as you scoop it up.

As you come up, bring your other hand across to ensure a strong hold.

Grab the ball with both hands as you look for options up the field.

Cyril Rioli's Footy Tip #2

THE SMOTHER

The smother can be a game-changer.

Thrust your hands from the hip across the direction of the kick.

Keep your hands together and your fingers spread.

Keep your eyes on the ball and do not raise your arms above your head.

Be sure to bring your hands down on the ball, not your opponent's foot.

Cyril Rioli's Footy Tip #3

THE BLIND TURN

The blind turn or pirouette is a great way to create space
and launch attacks from any part of the ground.

CYRIL RIOLI'S FOOTY TIP #3

Plant your foot firmly as you step to the side of your opponent.

Swing away from your opponent as you begin to turn to the side.

Continue to turn in, keeping low and holding the ball tightly.

Begin to accelerate away before straightening up.

ACKNOWLEDGEMENTS

It's a great thrill to have the second *Fox Swift* book released and I would like to thank the publisher, Geoff Slattery, for making this happen.

What can I say about Cyril Rioli? Even though he continues to destroy Essendon every time he plays against them, I can't look away. He is an out-and-out superstar of the AFL yet has the humility of a D-Grade Amateur, making him the perfect role model for young kids. It was fantastic teaming up with him again.

A very special thanks to Joey Gill (a.k.a. Lewis) for her brilliant drawings. The book just doesn't seem like a book until I see Joey's cartoons in there—they add such an important (and funny) layer to *Fox Swift*. I hope they will inspire lots of kids to draw.

To my editor, Bronwyn Wilkie—it is a joy to work with someone who not only understands me, but understands a better version of me. ("What I *think* you meant to say there, David, was …") 'BeeDub' smoothed out my often poorly arranged sentences and always came up with creative suggestions and solutions—an absolute gem.

To the group of young readers I road-tested the book on, thanks (in no particular order) to Sophie, Molly, Xander, Sammy, Louis, S-Dawg (Sarah), Rosie (who was the inspiration for Rosie McHusky), Sammy, Toby, Jack, Sam, Harry, Angus, Louis, Charlie and Ella.

ACKNOWLEDGEMENTS

A big shoutout to my (much) older sister Liz, who gave me such excellent feedback and suggestions throughout the writing process (cheque's in the mail!). To Mum and Dad, thanks once again for all the coffees, meals and support as I wrote *Fox Swift Takes on The Unbeatables* at your place on weekends. You are the Gary Ablett of parents.

A huge thank-you to all the kids who sent in ideas and supportive emails. There is nothing better than receiving a message from someone who has enjoyed reading your book. Massive respect! And I would like to give a special mention to the kids at Urquhart Park P.S., Forest Street P.S. and Sebastopol P.S. in Ballarat, where I met a number of creative writers (and sports stars) who will one day become household names.

Thanks to the whole team at Slattery Media Group— so much goes into putting a book together and then marketing it, and all your time and effort is greatly appreciated. And thanks also to the bookstores that have supported *Fox Swift* so well. Cyril, Jo and I want to encourage as many reluctant readers to read as we can, and it really helps when you have as many industry people behind you as possible.

Finally, to my family and friends who have put up with my unavailability while writing the book—I am officially back! Look forward to catching up soon.

DAVID LAWRENCE

David Lawrence is a comedy writer whose TV credits include *Talkin' 'Bout Your Generation*, *TV Burp* and *Hamish & Andy*. He runs the successful comedy business Laughing Matters with Jo Gill, is the author of the first *Fox Swift* book and the co-author with Eloise Southby-Halbish of *Anna Flowers*. David's goal was to play 100 games with Essendon, but due to a general lack of ability, he currently remains stranded on 0.

JO GILL

Jo Gill is a comedy writer and performer whose credits include *Hey Hey It's Saturday*, *Talkin' 'Bout Your Generation*, *Comedy Inc.*, *Hamish & Andy*, *Comic Relief*, and three years as head writer for the Logies. Jo has never won a Brownlow Medal, but has drawn three of them.

CYRIL RIOLI

Cyril Rioli has played more than 100 games and kicked more than 150 goals for the Hawthorn Football Club. He was a member of Hawthorn's premiership-winning team in 2008, his debut year in the AFL, and again in 2013.

WHAT'S NEXT FOR FOX?

Send us your ideas on how
Fox should spend his next
adventure ...

askus@foxswift.com.au

Keep up with the adventures of Fox Swift at

www.foxswift.com.au

If you like Fox Swift's

adventures against

The Unbeatables,

see where the story began!

Order at

www.foxswift.com.au

The story doesn't end here!
You can see what Fox Swift
is up to next in
Fox Swift and the Golden Boot!

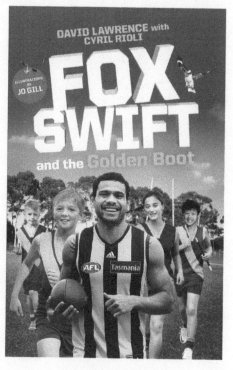

Order at
www.foxswift.com.au

AUTOGRAPHS

AUTOGRAPHS

AUTOGRAPHS

AUTOGRAPHS